MAROONED WITH A MARQUIS

EMILY E K MURDOCH

To Sophie and Dave – two of my favourite people.
And always, Joshua.

ACKNOWLEDGMENTS

This was the series that I never thought I could publish, so first thanks must go to my amazing Kickstarter supporters! Thank you for your faith in me, and I hope you love this book as much as I do!

Thank you to my wonderful editor, Julia Underwood, who has given me unparalleled advice – any mistakes left are completely my own!

Thank you to my glorious cover designer, Samantha Holt, a true artist whose patience with me is much appreciated.

Thank you to my ingenious formatter, Falcon Storm, whose willingness to format whenever I drop an unexpected email is fantastic!

And to my family. Thank you.

CHAPTER 1

*I*t was not until it was far too late that Adena Garland realised her mistake.

The afternoon had started well, at least. The sun had been gloriously warm and tempted her from Rowena Kerr's home to stroll along the beach, just one day since she had arrived from London. Adena's green gown wafted in the wind, and after checking around her to see that she was truly alone, she slipped off the shoes and stockings that were preventing her from delving her toes into the sand and stones.

She lost all track of time. The warm afternoon had brought her outside, and the beach seemed to tempt her onwards, ever onwards, until Rowena's house was out of sight, and she had meandered around another bend, and another bend. There was always another view to see, something else to discover.

And it was only as the sun resolutely turned around and started to dive slowly into the ocean, throwing up the most enchanting colours, that Adena turned to look back at her path home, and realised that the Kerrs' home had disappeared.

"Where is…" She murmured under her breath. Speaking aloud to herself had always been a rather strange habit her mother had tried to force out of her, but it was difficult, especially when she was completely alone as she was now on this strange beach, to resist the audible commentary. "Where did it go?"

'It' was the beach. While she had, but twenty minutes ago, walked along the stony sand quite happily, now that she turned back to return to the house, it was gone.

"The tide," Adena whispered, clutching her light shawl around her in nervous panic. "The tide must have come in and cut me off!"

She glanced around hurriedly now, looking for a route back to the mainland; but the tide had moved quickly, quicker than she could have imagined, and it had swallowed up her pathway entirely.

Adena made an irritated sound. "Well, that is just typical of you, is it not, Adena?"

Who would forget to keep an eye on the tide? Her muslin gown was warm enough in the heat of the day, but the sun was setting fast, and taking with it that balmy and pleasant glow. A chilling breeze swept around her face, tugging at the fiery red curls she had pinned up that morning.

It was most infuriating, of course, that she had only come to visit Rowena for a rest! The bustle and busyness of town had become so irritating, so tiring, that eventually she had decided that the country was the place for her, and Rowena's parents' home really could only be described as 'isolated'.

Built in the middle of nowhere, with the tiny village of Marshurst the only inhabitants for miles around – and that little place only consisting of ten to twelve families, at most – Rowena's invitation to visit could not have come at a better time.

It had taken just five minutes for Adena to send off her reply in a hastily written note, and two days for her to arrive. But as all was not well at the Kerrs, she found herself wandering further and further from the house in an attempt to lose herself: both from her familial duties in London, and the cares of the Kerrs. Rowena's frequent absences, her strange vague answers when her parents enquired where she had been – having a stranger in the house may keep the arguments to a quiet volume, but there were still bubbling under the surface, nonetheless.

And she had done just that. Now she was truly lost, far more lost than she had ever hoped to be, and there was no way back.

"This is just like you." She spoke quietly to herself as her head moved frantically this way and that, attempting to take in all that she was seeing. "Here you are, hoping to get away from civilisation for just ten days, and now you are trapped on an island that twenty minutes ago, did not even exist."

Of course, such natural phenomena existed. Just look at the Portland Bill, further along the coast: that became an island every day, and then reattached itself to the mainland as the tide turned. Look at St Michael's Mount. Sometimes you can cross to the island on foot, and sometimes on a boat.

"Yes, but those were proper islands," Adena reminded herself aloud. "With houses, and roads, and people. This is just a sandbank. A medley of sand, rocks, and a little vegetation."

Adena bit her lip. This was not the time to panic. This must happen to people all the time: it must do. It simply was not possible that she was the first to find herself completely stranded, and alone.

The panic that she had so far managed to keep at bay started to rise in her throat.

"What am I supposed to do, stay here all night?" She said to herself, trying to keep her voice calm and level, and failing. "To be sure, it is not an inhospitable place."

Her unusual green eyes glanced around her. A little scrubland, two or three trees…and sand. Lots of sand and rocks. This island, for now it could truly be described as such, was not much to look at, and would barely give her enough shelter for the night.

"Shelter for the night?" Adena repeated her thought aloud, and laughed bitterly. "'Tis not as though you have much choice, Miss Garland!"

Walking a few more yards, Adena saw with her own eyes that it was impossible; the rushing tide had made her a captive of this island, and there was nothing else for it.

She would be staying the night. Unless the Kerrs thought to look for her here, but she had mentioned to no one her desire for a solitary ramble.

Hunger that she had not noticed and thirst that

she had not regarded now overwhelmed her. Was she to go without?

"Options," she muttered to herself, glancing up and down the disappearing beach. "I need options."

Adena swallowed. This was not the type of holiday she had expected.

"Option one," she said decidedly, as she walked back towards where the beach had been, but the waves were now lapping at her toes. "I try to walk back to the shore. The tide may have come in, that is true, but it cannot be that deep in such a short amount of time, and I am likely to make it."

Likely, she thought quietly. Not the resounding confidence she had hoped for.

"Option two," Adena turned on the spot, and looked at the scrub, heathland, and few trees on the hastily forming island. "I attempt to find some shelter here, just for a few hours, and wait for the tide to turn."

But how long could that take? Six hours? Perhaps longer, and she did not fancy attempting to find the Kerrs' home in the dark, on her own.

Adena looked at the sun. It had touched the horizon now, and the air was definitely starting to cool. The flimsy shawl that she had taken with her as a matter of habit was not keeping her warm in the slightest.

"Option three," she said finally. "I try and stay the night here."

She swallowed again. It was not a particularly attractive concept, when you considered the lack of shelter, water, or food.

Three options: each as least as unlikely to be enjoyable – or successful – as the others. Adena clenched her fists and let the irritation with herself come to a boiling heat. She would need that anger.

"Well," she said decidedly, grabbing her forest green skirts and striding towards the waves. "There is just one thing for it."

LUKE, Marquis of Dewsbury watched the trickle of a wave break over his leather boots; watched the salty water give it a gleaming sheen, and then disappear back into the ocean, retreating from him as quickly as it came.

The ocean had always fascinated him, even as a child. His childhood home was nowhere near the sea, and so it was as a small child on an excursion that he first came across it, and it had bewitched his mind ever since.

And this was his favourite beach. He stood here, coloured golden in the setting sun, as the tide encroached upon the shore. He knew this tide: knew it better than most of the locals, he had visited so often. It often startled visitors to Marshurst, of course, as the quickening waters seemed to completely cut a person off from the mainland.

Luke laughed, remembering the first time that he had been 'stranded' on what the locals called Squire's Isle. He could still taste the bile at the back of his throat when he thought that he would have to remain there overnight, but as any local would tell you, if you wandered around the southern corner, you would easily find the path to the mainland.

His attention drifted from the waves, and Luke started to walk listlessly, too consumed by his thoughts to consider much else. The letter clenched in his hand was enough to draw his thoughts continuously.

So, Alexander, Duke of Caershire, was to be married. It should not have come as a surprise to him, he knew that. He had seen it coming from a mile away – before old Caershire himself. But to have it in writing, to see the invitation in black ink, the day, the time, the church…

Well, was there anything more final?

Luke grimaced at the thought of it. That made three: three of his bachelor friends this year had decided to shackle themselves to a woman – though thankfully, not the same woman, he thought with a grin.

The sea breeze ruffled his chestnut hair, getting too long now, he thought ruefully. He would have to visit his barber before he attended the wedding.

Wedding. Was there anything more constricting, more confining? Luke stared out across the sea, open and free, and shook his head sadly. There was no talking George or Alexander out of these marriages, he knew that, but he had expected – what? Better?

His mind cast back over the debutantes he had met, danced with, flirted with. They were countless, and they flickered across his memory as the dying sun flashed across the water.

None of them had ever brought him to temptation. Luke grinned wolfishly. Well, not a marital temptation, anyway. Plenty of nice dark corners in Almacks, after all. It would have been a shame to waste them.

And yet no marriage, and not for the lack of elderly mothers and well-meaning companions' attempts. Whether it was hints by letter, meaningful looks, or in the case of Lady Vaughan, a direct order to propose to her granddaughter, Luke had managed to escape them all.

Luke kicked at a stone that dropped heavily into the shallows. And where had all of that restraint brought him? Here, on Squire's Isle, completely alone, and with no one.

Or so he had thought. As he came around the next corner, his eyes became transfixed by the sight of an astonishing woman.

Red fiery hair was tumbling down her back, and she was standing in the ocean with her green gown flowing about her as though she was a mermaid. But this was no heavenly creature from the depths: this was a real woman.

"Damnit!"

He heard the cry uttered from the lady, and grinned despite himself. She may have the appearance of a mermaid, but she was evidently unaware of the route back to the mainland: trapped here, or so she thought, she must be trying to…walk back?

Luke's smile widened. Her silhouette against the setting sun really was most spectacular: a slender waist, and by the looks of it, a splendid posterior, better than any he had seen at St James'. My, to think that she was here, all alone – and he could rescue her.

Thrusting off his boots, Luke strode into the chilling water and called out, "Do not fear, I am coming to rescue you!"

The woman turned around, and Luke gasped aloud to see her. What perfection: skin smooth and pale, eyes that were as deep green as her soaking gown, with cheeks pink with the effort of forcing herself through the water, and a look of such ire that he almost stumbled.

"I – I am almost with you," he managed to say, though why he hardly knew. To think that he should find such a woman here, at the back of beyond! He would have to keep himself under control, for there was never such a woman who had got his blood as hot as this.

It was only when he reached out to grab her hand, and the strange woman screamed and tried to shake him off, that Luke realised that his calling out probably did not reach her. The wind was blowing towards the shore, and so she probably had no prior warning that he was behind her.

"Get off me – help!" She cried out, eyes desperately searching for someone, anyone to rescue her from this madman.

Just my luck, thought Luke irritably as he held onto her. Of course: that much beauty, why would anyone care to develop a personality?

"If you would just hold still," he said aloud in a dry voice, "I can get us both to land."

The struggling stopped, and those dazzling unusual green eyes flashed at him suspiciously. "The mainland?"

For a moment, Luke hesitated. Looking back as he did, years later, he could still not entirely understand what made him say those next words. They just crept out of him, as though he was following a line from a play.

All he knew was that he would never forgive himself if he did not give himself a chance to get to know this mysterious woman better...and what better way to entice conversation than to be trapped on an island together?

And after all, Luke reasoned with himself silently as she stared at him, awaiting his answer. It was just for one night.

"No," he said decidedly. "'Tis too far to the mainland – we have to go back to the Squire's Isle.

The island," he added, at the mystified look on her face. "At any rate, we cannot stand here."

The rising cold in his legs was starting to make his teeth chatter, as the rising tide had brought the sea over his knees – and she was shivering, glaring as she was at him as though deciding whether to believe him, or try and swim to shore!

"I do not …" she began, but Luke had had enough.

In a quick strong sweeping motion, he threw one arm around her shoulders and the other dived into the water and lifted below her knees.

The piercing scream that emanated from his captive echoed across the water, but Luke knew that it would never reach the ears of anyone. The two figures that he had seen walking along the beach had long gone, and no matter how much she struggled, his grip on her was firm.

A little too firm. Luke swallowed, and tried to relax his grip a little while still holding onto her, preventing her from escaping him. By God, but if he had met her in town then things could have been very different. He could feel the softness of her, and her breasts heaved close to his eyes as he struggled to carry the heaviness of her damp gown.

After taking two steps on dry land, Luke gently lowered the woman to a standing position.

"Well!" She exploded, glaring at him. "I suppose you think that is very impressive, but now what are we going to do?"

CHAPTER 2

*a*dena stared at the strange man, heat rising in her cheeks. This was absolutely ridiculous: who did he think he was, manhandling her like that? It was enough to make her scream.

"Do?" The man blinked at her. "What do you mean, do?"

"You may not have noticed," said Adena furiously, pointing a finger at the sky, "but it is almost night time. I would have preferred to spend the evening in a comfortable bed, but apparently you thought that I would rather sleep on sand?"

No matter how much she glared at him, the strange man did not seem to be concerned by her look of anger – and the more that she looked at him, and her cheeks flamed even deeper as the thought crossed her mind, the more she noticed just how handsome he was. Tall, with chestnut hair that was a little too long to be fashionable, broad shoulders and a grin that none of her words seemed to have wiped from his face.

"My dear lady, you really think that you would have been able to stride through the waters to the mainland?" He smirked at her. "Not possible, I am afraid. If anything, you should be thanking me."

"Thank – thanking you?" Adena spluttered. It was fortunate that the evening was so warm, or else she would surely be shivering.

"It is absolutely my pleasure," said the gentleman – if gentleman he was, which Adena wanted to doubt but could not, taking in the expensive clothes that he was wearing. "Please, it was my pleasure."

"I am not thanking you, I am furious with you!" Adena glared at him, and then strode a few yards down the beach. "To think that I am stuck here on this – what did you call it?"

The gentleman bowed to her, and said, "Squire's Isle."

"Squire's Isle indeed," she muttered, staring around what was going to be her home for the next few hours. "You had no right to take me from the sea, and to…to carry me."

It was only as she said those words that the memory of him carrying her flooded back into her mind, and Adena's cheeks, flushed before due to rage, now flushed from heated embarrassment. There had been so much strength in his arms, she had never felt more securely held, or more safe. How could a man that she had only just met give her such a feeling?

Trying to put aside the pleasant feeling of security and safety, Adena glanced at the man once more, and was suddenly overtaken when she noticed his wet shirt clinging to his chest. The flush deepened, and he smiled at her.

"My dear lady, if I had not plucked you from the waters, you would have undoubtedly drowned. There is a deep ravine just a few yards before you that would have prevented you from walking, and," taking a step towards her and smiling, "I do not think with such an elegant gown you would have been able to swim."

"Ravine? Here? Surely not." Adena took an automatic step backwards as he came towards her.

The man's smile deepened. "You could say that I saved your life."

"Are you expecting me to thank you?" Adena shot back, more bravely than she felt. Why, she was completely at this man's mercy.

The man tilted his head slightly and looked her up and down. "You look like a gentlewoman, and so yes. I would expect some sort of gratitude."

It was most infuriating, Adena decided silently, that this odious man was so handsome. It was all too easy to be charmed by him, she was sure, but she would not allow mere good looks to dazzle her.

Still. If what he was saying was true, she certainly owed her life to him. How provoking.

"I suppose," she said, ungraciously. "Thank you. Now tell me, when does the tide go out?"

The man hesitated, and then said, "Hours. Eight or nine?"

Adena's shoulders slumped, and she bit her lip. Well, there was nothing for it then.

"We have nowhere to go," she said quietly. "We are both stuck here – and you should know better, I would say, by your knowledge of the tides – but there is nothing else for it."

The gentleman raised an eyebrow.

"We will have to stay here overnight," explained Adena with a wry smile. "I hope that you do not mind having me as a companion?"

For a moment, it looked as though he was going to retort that he very much minded. He stared at her, as though attempting to commit her features to memory, and Adena found herself all of a sudden very conscious that her damp gown was clinging rather scandalously to certain parts of her body that probably did not need additional emphasis.

And then that winning smile appeared on his face again, and he bowed. "Luke…Northmere, at your service."

Adena rolled her eyes. You would have thought, in the circumstances, that they could have dispensed with the ceremony, but society's rules had to be obeyed – even if civilisation was a long way off.

She dropped into a deep curtsey, and murmured, "Adena Garland."

When she rose, she found that Mr Northmere had taken another step forward. Her eyes widened and she tried not to show her surprise.

"Northmere," she repeated slowly. "I know that name."

That certainly seemed to startle him. He stopped abruptly, and the seemingly ever present smile disappeared from his face.

"Have you?" He said, rather roughly. "All good things, I hope?"

Adena was trying desperately to think where she had seen the name before, and then she remembered. "Is not your brother getting married soon? I am sure that I saw the notice of it recently, in the paper."

The tension in his face relaxed, and he nodded briefly. "That is correct, my brother George."

It was quite evident to Adena that he was neither cheered nor pleased with this remembrance of hers. So, he was not in favour of matrimony then? Well, that was at least one thing that they had in common.

"Pardon?"

Adena flushed. Had she said that last part aloud? It certainly looked that way. Mr Northmere was staring at her with a slightly confused expression on his face, but there was the threat of a smile there also. Did this man ever stop smiling?

"I simply thought – 'tis of no matter," she said hastily, and tried to smile. Something about the way that he was looking at her, or perhaps it was his close proximity to her, was starting to unnerve her. "I hope that you will not miss the nuptials due to your imprisonment by nature here."

He stared at her, and Adena felt a rush of heat flow through her again – but this was not embarrassment. He looked as though he could undress her with his eyes, and she was horrified to find that she was slightly enjoying it.

"Well then, Miss Garland," Mr Northmere said, smiling. "Best foot forward."

Luke attempted to control his gaze as they walked slowly along the beach, but it was difficult. Now that Miss Adena Garland was out of the water, it was impossible not to notice three things.

Firstly, that she was not wearing any shoes, and the brief flashes of ankle as her gown moved was starting to distract him.

Secondly, that the fiery hues of her hair were just as present in her temper, and he was startled to find that he revelled in provoking her.

Thirdly, that she was the most intoxicatingly beautiful woman that he had ever met, and his body was not letting him forget it.

Even in the silence that they were walking in, his body was crying out to him to reach out to her, to take her arm, to hold her hand, to do anything that would bring his flesh in contact with hers.

No. He would have to control that particular

desire: he may be a man with few morals in that area, and he may have bedded a few women in his time, but not like this. Not when she was helpless, protectorless, and trapped on what she thought was an island.

A smile of pleasure crept over his face. By God, he would have given his back teeth for an excuse like this with Miss Garland – the perfect opportunity to act as protector, guide, and finally, lover.

"…do not you think?"

Luke started as Miss Garland's words cut through his thoughts, and he shook his head as though ridding his water from his ears to try and concentrate on her words.

She had stopped and was staring at him. "Have you been listening to a word I have said?"

Luke decided on brutal honesty. After all, it was not as though they would ever meet again after this night. "No, I am afraid not, Miss Garland."

She visibly bristled, and he found a delicate rush of pleasure echo through his body. My, but it really was too easy to infuriate this woman – and what a shame for her that her beauty only heightened in her frustration.

"I *said*," glaring at him with emphasis, "that as the sun's rays will almost certainly be gone in the next twenty minutes, do you not think that we should find some shelter, and light a fire?"

Luke glanced around him. The idea of snuggling up with Miss Adena Garland was definitely a delicious prospect, but he doubted that she had the same intention.

"There are a few trees here," he said decidedly. "And my pocketknife. Let us see what we can make of them."

Miss Garland rolled her eyes. "How very intrepid of you. Come on then."

It took them but a minute to reach the scrub and trees, and Luke could see by her face that she was downcast.

"There is enough here for firewood," she said quietly, "but not a shelter."

"Oh, I would not say that," Luke found himself speaking with an encouraging air. "You sit there, Miss Garland, and hum a ditty under your breath. I shall be back shortly."

She glared at him for a moment, as though attempting to catch him in irreverence, but seeing as she could do little else, she dropped to the stony sand.

Luke frowned to himself. It was all very impressive of him to rescue her from the sea, and a very clever thought of him to hide the fact that the 'Isle' was still attached to the mainland, but they were both damp, and likely to get colder as the night went on. What had he been thinking? Did he think that she would throw herself into his arms the moment that they reached the shore, kiss him passionately as thanks, relinquish herself to his desires, and then happily trot back to the mainland with him as he 'discovered' the way home, all in time for brandy by ten o'clock?

"And what are you going to do?" Miss Garland's voice once again interrupted his thoughts, but this time they were softly spoken, and there was no anger in her eyes.

"I," said Luke decidedly, "am going to surprise you. Stay there."

There was nothing for it now, after all, Luke decided. They could discover the way home together in the morning, and it wasn't a bad way to spend an evening: with a beautiful woman, huddled under a shelter together.

Luke swallowed. He would have to be far more controlled in reality than in his thoughts.

It took him only five minutes of searching to find what he was looking for. A heavy branch, covered in leaves, had fallen from its trunk not two weeks past, by the look of the seaweed clumped around it. Luke could almost remember the storm that had lashed on London window panes. Heaving it over his shoulders, and cursing slightly at the ruined shirt that he was sure would never recover from sand, salt, and now soil, he half carried, half dragged it back to where he had left Miss Garland.

She was sitting knees hugged to her chest as she glanced round to watch him approach.

"What do you have there?"

"Shelter," Luke panted, slightly disconcerted at the strain that he was having to put in to pull the heavy branch towards her.

Leaping up, she moved out of the way in the growing gloomy darkness, and stared as he pulled the branch and leaned it carefully against two trees that had grown against each other.

It was not perfect, and Luke would have been the first to admit that. But it was shelter, of a sort, and Adena crept underneath it with a small smile.

"I must admit, I am impressed," she said, glancing up at him. "Who would have known, to look at you, that you had such ingenious ideas up your sleeve?"

"All the more impressive when you learn that I was not born for this manual life," said Luke breezily, dropping down beside her and finding to his own astonishment that he was but three inches from her.

At first, she had shrunk back, but seeing that he was going to move no closer, Miss Garland relaxed and looked at him curiously. "What sort of life were you born for, then?"

He did not answer immediately. Instead, he took in the blazing red hair flowing down her back in waves; it contrasted beautifully with her green gown, which was still damp and clung alluringly across her breasts and hips. She sat there, as though unaware of her beauty, and the very tangible effects that it was having on his own body.

Well, there was no point in hiding it.

"You may have heard of me by another name," Luke said with a devilish smile. "At least, I almost hope you have. I am Luke Northmere, but I am also the eldest son of the Duke of Northmere, making me, the Marquis of Dewsbury."

If he had a particular response in mind, hers was not it. Miss Garland's eyes widened, and then she smiled wryly. "Well, that is something. Do I need to curtsey again, or will my former effort suffice?"

Luke was not a vain man: not compared to most of his station, anyway. But he was accustomed to a little more deference shown when his title was revealed, and in some cases, coquettish smiles, and tilts of the head, and a stretch of the body to show off one's waist.

Not this ironic grin that he was faced with now, as those green eyes stared at him mercilessly.

"Yes," he managed, "I mean, no. I just thought you ought to know, that was all."

But Miss Garland was not going to let him get away with it that easily. "No, you wanted a response, did you not, my lord? For that is how I must address you now, as you well know. Did you hope for a blushing sigh? A gentle lean," and here she moved closer to him, and his breath caught in his throat, "so that I could be closer to you?"

Luke opened his mouth, but no sound came out. Really, this was stupid: he was hardly a fresh faced boy of sixteen!

Miss Garland laughed, and leaned back. "I apologise, my lord, I can see that you are not one to be teased. But really, when you have moved in society as I have, you start to weary of dukes and lords and titles. Why, I am here hiding from my very own future title!"

At those words, she clapped slender fingers over her lips, and her eyes widened.

Luke grinned. "Ah, now we get to the truth of it: you are engaged to be married, then, and to a gentleman of rank!"

There was something in her expression that told him she had not meant to impart such information, but she bore it well, and said nothing more than, "Never you mind. At this moment, all that concerns me is that I am marooned with a marquis."

CHAPTER 3

The laugh that Luke managed did not ring true to his ears, but Miss Adena Garland seemed satisfied. Her gaze slipped off him, and moved to the now almost invisible ocean that they could hear slowly crashing against the shore-line, but could barely see in the evening twilight.

Luke coughed, and shifted himself on the soil. If he was honest with himself – and it was not a position that he liked to be in, to be sure – he would have to admit that he was now starting to care a little too much about Miss Garland's opinion of him.

Sweeping her off her feet in the sea, winning smiles, building a shelter: his attempts to show off were juvenile, and his face flushed in the growing darkness when he considered his actions.

He would expect just such silliness from a pup of eighteen, about to attend his first ball and desperately hoping to secure the card of the most eligible lady in the room.

Not from Luke, Marquis of Dewsbury and contented bachelor.

"Marooned?" He said in what he had hoped with a joking tone, but there was a little quiver in it as he tried not to glance over at the woman beside him. "Yes, I suppose we are. 'Tis rather like an adventure novel, do not you think?"

There was no answer but a shrug from his companion.

Attempting to make light of the situation and her comment had not worked. Luke felt the searing heat of jealousy flow into his heart as he saw her complete non-interest in his words. Of course she would not, he told himself. She is engaged to another, and does not have the time nor the inclination to favour you with her smiles.

Luke could not help it. He tilted his head slightly so that he could look at Miss Garland; the curve of her neck as she stared out towards the ocean, the way she had buried her feet into the sandy soil, the red hair, curling even more now that it was starting to dry.

What was he doing, allowing himself to – what, feel something for this woman? It was ridiculous to feel jealous of a man whom he did not know and possibly had never met.

And after all, had he not decided against marriage? Was it not his constant irritation, these last few weeks, that the great and the good of his acquaintance were succumbing to the temptations of the marriage bed without any thought for the decades of trials and tribulations to come?

A seagull squawked overhead, and Miss Garland looked upwards, a smile breaking across her face. Luke's stomach twisted horribly, and yet it sent a jolt of heat towards his pelvis.

What was he getting himself into?

Luke jumped up. "I am going to see what improvements can be made to our shelter," he said hastily.

Miss Garland barely looked round, her eyes were still transfixed on the sky seeing if she could espy the bird above them.

Luke cleared his throat. "Miss Garland, I will be leaving you for a short while."

Why did he care so much for her response?

Why did it matter to him so much that she noticed his leaving, that she was interested in his actions – perhaps, responded to him?

"I will be back shortly," he said in a brusque voice, and turned away before he heard the reply he realised he was desperate for.

"And I am going for a short walk," said a gentle voice, with none of the ire remaining in it. "I feel the need for a little stroll, and I hope that my gown will dry a little with the movement."

It struck Luke that the quickest way to dry out the gown was to remove it, and suspend it over a fire, but he was not going to spark the anger of Miss Garland with such a suggestion.

"That is an excellent idea," he said instead, but as he watched her rise in the night air, he added, "Miss Garland, you must take this. Here."

Luke shrugged off his greatcoat, and held it out to her. If he had known her well – if she had been a friend of the family, perhaps, or a woman that he had known for many years in society – then she would have stepped towards him, turned with a coy smile, and allowed him to drape the greatcoat over her shoulders. There would have been a moment of intimacy, of flirtation, of suggesting what could be.

Not so with Miss Garland. She outstretched a

hand to take it from him, and refusing to take a step closer, could not reach it.

Luke smiled, stepped forward, and allowed her to take it from him. For a split second, their fingers touched.

Her gasp was masked by his own, as heat and sparks seemed to move between them as her delicate skin touched his. It was like two magnets finding their home with each other; unlike anything Luke had ever experienced.

Throat dry, heart racing, his eyes moved from his fingers to her face. He saw in her expression the answer to his own: shock, surprise, and a little curiosity as to what could cause such a strong reaction.

"Thank you, my lord," she whispered, eyes not leaving his own.

Luke coughed, and nodded. "You are quite welcome, Miss Garland."

The first true smile that he had seen from her emerged slowly, and then she took a step forward and handed back his greatcoat.

"Perhaps you would be so good?"

He had never felt this way about a woman before him, Luke thought as he gently placed the greatcoat over her shoulders. His heart almost stopped beating, and he could hear his breathing heavy in his ears as he gently and almost reverentially gathered her hair together, placing it outside the greatcoat so that it fell, fire-like down her back.

She was so close. So very close that he could feel the icy chill of her, and was glad that he had thought to give her what little additional warmth he could offer her. Her breathing seemed irregular, and without stepping away from him, she tilted her head to look at him.

Her lips were pink, and glistening. She had just licked them, and Luke felt a stirring deep inside him that was definitely not gentlemanly.

"Thank you, my lord," Miss Garland whispered.

He could feel her breath on him, and he knew that all he had to do was move two inches, no more, and he would be kissing her. The temptation was overwhelming.

"I think, given the circumstances," he whispered back in a low voice, "that it would be quite acceptable for you to call me Luke."

For an instant, it looked as though she was going to censure him for impertinence; it was a very forward remark, and one that he would have been astonished at, if he had heard such intimacy in London.

But this woman was like no other.

"In that case," she murmured, and Luke attempted not to follow the elegant movement of her lips, "you should call me Adena. I hope you will."

"Adena," Luke breathed, and unable to resist any longer, moved forward.

But he moved too late; Adena had stepped forward, greatcoat now clutched around her body, and she smiled back at him as she went. "I will not stray too far, and your concern, bizarre and unwarranted as it is, is noted."

"Be careful," Luke found himself calling after her. "Do not wander too far from me, you may not find me again."

As she wandered into the darkness, Luke shook his head with a smile as though drunk. You may not find me again: did his desperation to be near her have to be quite so blatant? What had got into him? He had met many a pretty woman before, plenty of fiery, spirited women before, but had experienced nothing like this.

But not quite so stunning as her, he admitted to

himself. Nor so spirited, nor combining so much of spark and spirit in one woman.

The evening gloom had already swallowed up Miss Adena Garland – or Adena, as he now had permission to consider her. Luke grinned. They were a long way from the drawing rooms of the *ton*.

The smile faded as the thought struck him that she may find her way back to the mainland on her little excursion, or at the very least, see that there was a way back, despite his information. If she discovered his deception, she was unlikely to look at him with such a pleasing eye.

Luke shook his head, and started off in the opposite direction. In the unlikely event that she did, what was the problem? All he had to do was act as astonished and relieved as she was, and his surprise would completely hide his knowledge from her.

He almost stumbled over some gorse as a little needle of guilt pricked his conscience. What sort of a man was he that could happily lie to a woman – a woman whom he had never met before this evening, and who had put her life, her very reputation in his hands?

Without knowing the exact time, Luke estimated that it was almost thirty minutes later that he deemed his haul of large leaves and additional branches ready to be taken back to the initial shelter that he had started. His fingers were covered in dirt, there were at least two thorn scratches up his arms, and this shirt would never be the same again.

He had never worked so hard with his hands in his life, and he felt it. With an aching back and weary arms, Luke turned once more towards the shelter, and smiled ruefully.

If any of his friends could see him now, they would laugh at him just as much as he would have done, if he had watched another act in the way that he was. Why was he trying so hard to impress this woman?

Was it because the title, a mainstay in his wooing repertoire, seemed to have had absolutely no effect?

Was it because her beauty had completely dazzled him, to the point where he seemed unable to comprehend sense?

Or, said a small voice somewhere deep in his heart that he discovered to his surprise, was it because Adena was unlike any he had ever met, or was likely to meet – a truly unique woman. That sparkling wit that she started to reveal before she went on that walk of hers…

There was nothing else for it: Luke trudged back with his spoils, trying to ignore the aches and complaints of his body, and trying not to imagine Adena slowly removing that damp gown by a fireside.

She is engaged to another, he reminded himself. Engaged to another, and one with a title too, so there is no need to hope that she will be impressed by your own.

There was something strange up ahead that caused him to pause slightly in his return. It looked, to all intents and purposes, like a lamp: but that surely could not be. He could not be so unfortunate, Luke thought bitterly to himself, to find himself 'trapped' with Miss Adena Garland just to find that there was another man here out to get her too!

He was immediately overcome with shame. Out to get her?

The lamp light flickered, but as he took a few steps forward, it became clear that it was no lamp, but a fire. There was a figure standing beside it, tall and strong. Luke's heart sank. So, it was to be another gentleman joining them. Of course it was.

But then the figure moved, and Luke's breath caught in his throat. If he was not mistaken, that was no gentleman, but a lithe and elegant woman standing wearing his greatcoat by a fire.

Like a siren calling out to sailors to throw themselves towards her, a voice spoke out from the darkness.

"My lord? Luke, is that you?"

Luke tried to speak, but couldn't. He could refute his own feelings no longer: he was entranced by Miss Adena Garland, utterly taken in by her bodily charms. His own body yearned to rush over to her, abandoning all he had collected for the shelter, and sweep her into his arms, pouring down his passion and lack of restraint in hot kisses.

"Luke?"

"It is I," he managed in a strangled voice.

So. He had feelings, of a mingled lust and obsession sort, for this woman. 'Twas merely an infatuation, however, and he needed to guard his tongue and his temperament to ensure that the lady was not put to any trouble or awkwardness on his behalf.

Luke found himself smiling dryly. Turns out that he had plenty of honour left in him, but it had taken a strange encounter with a woman he had never clapped eyes on before this night to discover it.

CHAPTER 4

*A*dena stared out into the darkness. It had certainly looked like a figure, moving about in the darkness, and around about Luke – my lord Luke, she corrected herself silently, pulling his greatcoat closer around her.

But when she had called out, the figure had stopped short, just out of the glare of the fire she had managed to light.

"My lord?" She repeated, eyes straining to attempt to make out just who the figure was. "Luke, I shall be most displeased if that is you, and you are not stepping forward."

There was a deep laugh, and Luke strode into view, carrying with him what looked like half of the trees of the island.

"Your temper is quick to burn," he said with a smile. "Much like the fire – how on earth did it get here?"

A small wave of irritation flowed through Adena as she stared at him: shirt covered in leaves, a scratch across his face, and yet utter charm on his features. He really did think that he was something special, she thought. Such a shame that on the outside at least, he was right.

"Get here?" She said, raising an eyebrow. "Really, Luke, do you have any grasp of the elements of physics? Unless a very small and quiet lightning storm decided to hit us here on the – what did you call this?"

"Squire's Isle," he said, throwing down the heavy branches near the makeshift shelter that he had built.

Adena tried not to notice the rise and swell of the muscles through the linen shirt as she continued, "Squire's Isle, then I think the most reasonable thing to presume is that I lit the fire."

Luke swung around, and she almost laughed aloud to see the astonishment and confusion on his face.

"You – the fire, you lit the fire?"

A twig in the flames shifted, throwing dancing

light across his features, and something instinctual stirred inside Adena's breast. My, but he was handsome, it would be foolish to deny it. Adena had never seen a man so perfectly formed, and in body as well as face.

She nodded with a smile. "I lit the fire."

Luke moved slowly towards it, reaching out his hands to gain the full strength of its warmth on his fingers. Trying not to watch him too closely, Adena gently lowered herself onto the sandy soil, and gazed up at him.

"You had a tinder box on you, I suppose."

She shook her head, and then added as he was not looking at her, "No, not at all."

His head tilted down to look at her and she was suddenly overwhelmed with the feeling of just how strong he was: how masculine, how tall, how broad, and how utterly alone she was with him, in the deepening evening, on an island away from civilisation.

Anything could happen, she thought, and shivered at the unknowable excitement that flowed through her.

"No tinderbox?"

Adena smiled. "When I was growing up with two brothers, I very swiftly learned that unless I could run as fast as them, climb as high as them, and set fire to as much as they could, I was going to be left behind. No little sister wants that, and so I undoubtedly have a few skills in my gentlewoman's repertoire that I have never needed to display at Almacks."

Luke roared with laughter. "I can quite imagine you let loose in your father's garden, sticks in one hand and kindling in another."

"Oh, far more than that," a smile creeping over her face at the memory of it. "The garden almost merged with the parkland, and I am almost afraid to say that Kieran, Oliver, and I almost ran wild. There was nothing to stop us exploring for miles each day."

"No tutor? Governess?"

For a moment, Adena wondered at his interest in her, but ignored it. It was nice to be given attention, though it made her feel ridiculous to admit it, even to herself. It was unusual to just be listened to, without a chaperone at each elbow attempting to prod you into marriage.

"No adults of any kind," she answered, with relish. "I am sorry to say that I grew up totally wild, though my parents would always deny it."

There was a minute of silence as Luke's face

turned once again to the flames, and she was given the chance to examine his features closely. Dark hair, longer than most but still fashionable, with a trimmed beard across his face. Dark eyes: darker than any she had ever seen before, almost black, though that could have been the firelight. A strong mouth. A mouth of confidence. Being kissed by that mouth, and here Adena blushed but did not look away, would certainly be something.

"And so you are now a little firestarter," Luke said finally.

Adena laughed gently. "I suppose you could say that. I have rarely used the talent, and I am almost relieved that I still have the knack when I really needed it."

"Well, I must say that I am impressed," he admitted with a wry smile. "I had not thought it possible, I must say – and I am rarely impressed."

"That much I can believe," retorted Adena quietly, and she coloured slightly as he roared with laughter. "You were not supposed to hear that, my lord."

Still laughing, Luke threw himself down beside her and laid out, propping himself up on one elbow. "Oh, my lord this, my lord that – I think, given the circumstances, that we can dispense with that as well."

Something like a shiver moved through Adena's body as he spoke. Perhaps it was because he was so close to her. Perhaps it was because he stared so deeply into her eyes, not looking away, refusing to break the connection.

Whatever it was, it was intoxicating, and overwhelming, and she looked away.

"I must admit I am a little jealous of you," Luke said quietly, and though she had turned her eyes back to the fire, she could sense his gaze still on her.

"Jealous of me?" She managed.

He picked up a twig from the ground, and started to pull it apart with his fingers. "I was never that close with my brothers, of which I have several. No running about in the woodland tearing it up for firewood."

Adena was intrigued, despite herself. "How many brothers do you have?"

There was a pause, and she could not help but look round at him. "You are struggling to remember?"

She wished that she had taken back those words as soon as she had uttered them, when she saw the pain that swept across his features.

"I apologise," she said quickly, "I should not have – "

"There are four of us now," said Luke heavily, "but my mother had seven sons at one time."

Adena bit her lip. There she went, careering into a conversation with no thought for the consequences, and now she had evidently opened up old wounds.

"I am...I am so sorry," she murmured. "I should not have pried into your private – "

"Oh, do not concern yourself." Luke pulled himself up and sat, one leg stretched out and the other bent at the knee, next to her. "'Tis no great secret, half of society know about it, so it just happens that you are in the other half."

For a moment, Adena thought that the conversation had closed, but then the deep voice beside her continued.

"Simon died when we were very small. He must have been, what….five? George and Harry had not even been born then, he caught some sort of pox. Richard was fourteen when he was thrown from a horse in a hunt – that was terrible, the whole family was there, I do not think my mother truly recovered."

His voice was low, but it was steady. Adena

risked a glance at him, and though there was pain etched in his features, there was a sort of resoluteness in his eyes, as though now he had started to speak of them, there was no ending the conversation until it had run its course.

"But it was Magnus that was the true loss," Luke said heavily, and she heard the first quaver in his voice. "Our youngest, George, had been reading in the library with him, and his twin Harry had already gone up to bed. When George was leaving, he saw that Magnus had fallen asleep in his armchair – a common occurrence, for Magnus could sleep anywhere."

Adena saw the bitter smile creep over his face, and then disappear.

"George thought he would leave him the candle," Luke sighed heavily. "Poor soul, he could never have known what consequences that action would have. By the time that we realised the fire had spread through the library, through the drawing room, and up the stairs, it was impossible to get everyone out."

Horror filled Adena's heart and lungs. "Fire?"

He nodded.

"But I have just been boasting to you of my own

prowess with the flame," she said quietly, horrified at her own stupidity.

Luke wafted away her words with his hand. "How could you have known? And it is a skill, no matter what happened that night."

Adena swallowed. "So…so you lost Magnus that night."

He nodded gravely, and then a bitter smile appeared on his face, almost throwing his features into greater handsomeness. "Magnus, two maidservants, our butler who attempted to put out the flames…and my mother."

"Your mother!"

"She would not leave the house without her boys," said Luke, and it was now a genuine smile that Adena could see on his face. "She was, truly, the most loving mother. I was in town, as the eldest, and George had roused Harry and the others, taken them by a different route. As soon as my mother realised that Magnus was still inside, she broke free of my father and went back in."

Sympathy was pouring into Adena's heart almost in rhythm with the soft sweeping of the waves on the shore. "I am so sorry for your losses," she whispered.

Luke started, as though he had forgotten she was there. "Thank you."

Adena moved without even thinking, running on pure instinct. His hand was on his knee, and she reached out with her own and clasped it.

Perhaps it was all this talk of fire, but Adena gasped aloud at the heat from his hand that seared hers like a branding iron. At the same time, a flush of heat moved across her face and descended into her stomach, curling into a ball of warmth that felt strange, but not unwanted.

"Oh, Luke," she said, her breath caught in her throat.

LUKE ALMOST HAD to check that he had not thrust his hand into the fire, the feeling of flame was so real. But no: it was just Adena's hand.

Just Adena. How could he even think such a thing, feeling the warmth flowing from him as her touch inflamed him. Oh, if he only had the self-control not to feel this passion for her – or the complete lack of self-control to do something about it.

"I think I saw an abandoned fishing net over

there," he said hurriedly, drawing his hand away from hers and jumping upwards, as though putting a few feet between them would dampen down the heat that was rising in his body.

Luke glanced down at her, and was almost gratified to see a corresponding flush in her face. So, she felt it too.

"I will stay here and, and tend the fire," she managed to say before Luke strode off into the darkness.

This was complete madness, he told himself. Madness! He was the Marquis of Dewsbury, he could not go around hoping to seduce another man's fiancée!

Every step took him into greater darkness, but the memory of her face in the light, the firelight making her hair look even more fiery than it already was, that look of intensity that she had given him as their hands had touched –

Luke could feel the physical effects on his body, and stretched his shoulders irritably. With every other young woman he met, he had had complete self-control – and now this Adena Garland had removed all ability for him to calm himself!

He did not find the net again, but instead tripped right over it. Cursing into the darkness and hoping beyond hope that Adena had not seen him, he threw the net into the ocean and threw himself down onto the damp sand to wait.

It could have been five minutes, or an hour, he could not tell, but eventually he heard the splashing that indicated a fish had been trapped in the net. Not one, two. Pulling it in, he enwrapped the struggling fish in the net and strode back towards the glint of the fire in the distance.

"Luke?"

He smiled. It felt good to hear her call out his name like that. Now, if only he could have her crying out his name for quite a different reason...

The power of his imagination rocked him, stopping him in his tracks. No, he told himself firmly. No. You have taken this island deception far enough: you will not touch her, for she is at your mercy.

Or I am at hers, he thought wryly as Adena once more came into sight.

"What do you have there?" She had not moved from the spot where he had left her, it seemed, but she looked pleased to see him. "Oh, those poor fish – why have you not put them out of their misery?"

Luke glanced down at them, and saw the two fish still wriggling in the net. "Oh, I – "

"Come here," said Adena firmly, holding out her hand so decidedly that he did not question her.

After taking the net with the struggling fish entangled in it, Luke watched as she picked up a heavy stone, carefully aimed, and –

"There," she said matter-of-factly. "Do you have a penknife, or something, to gut them?"

Luke laughed, and shook his head. "Nay, my lady, for you truly are a lady of complete wonder to me. 'Tis you that has the penknife, it is in my pocket here."

What a woman. She certainly had not been exaggerating when she said that she ran wild with her brothers. Luke watched, fascinated, as she carefully drew out the guts of the fish and threw them into the fire, causing it to smoke a little.

"There," she said finally, glancing up at Luke with a nervous smile on her face. "Have I shocked you sufficiently yet?"

Tempting as it was to give his real opinion of her, which was that he wanted to utterly possess her for a good few hours into the night, Luke nodded with a smile. "Now, will you let me cook them?"

He had no idea what possessed him to offer; the last time he had cooked fish on a fire, he had been but thirteen and even then, he had done it badly.

Perhaps it was seeing just how independent she was. Perhaps it was time for him to contribute something to their little wilderness.

Within minutes, the regret was complete. He had no idea how it was possible that the outside of the fish were burned but the inside was still raw, but he persevered in silence, and tried not to notice those dark green eyes watching his every movement.

She felt something. He knew that she did, no one could react like that to someone's touch and not feel something. But what was it: intrigue, interest, lust?

And dare he find out?

"There, that should do it," he said hopefully after what must have been another twenty minutes. "I am afraid that my dining service is a little lax this evening, but I hope you will not mind."

Adena smiled at him, and reached out her hands for the partly charred fish, flinching slight at its heat. Though he could not have said why, Luke was careful that he did not touch her skin again.

Throwing himself down beside her, and perhaps a little closer than was necessary, Luke took his own fish and made an exploratory bite.

There was no use beating about the bush: it was disgusting. Attempting not to gag, Luke forced half of it down, knowing that he would be glad to have something in his stomach when morning came, and hoped beyond hope that the other fish was some-what better.

By the look of Adena's face, it was just as repul-sive – but she caught his eye, and smiled. "Thank you for the fish, Luke, it really...it really is delicious."

Luke was not sure what made him happier: the fact that she was lying to him to prevent his feelings from being hurt, or the flirtatious way that she did it.

"You are the worst liar I have ever met," he said with a broad grin, and to his utter surprise, Adena burst into giggles.

"And you are the worst cook I have ever met!"

Luke stared at her, and then joined her laughter. "I am sure that there is someone out there worse than I!"

"I cannot think how!" Adena's laugh reached to her eyes, which were fixed on his own. "My good-ness, Luke, how can you eat that?"

Grinning broadly, Luke swept out the remainder of his fish, and threw it spectacularly into his mouth – or it would have been into his mouth, if it had not disintegrated into chunks of badly cooked or overly burnt fish which rained down on him.

His look of surprise must have been hilarious, for Adena was clutching her sides with laughter.

Thankfully, Luke was able to see the funny side. Joining with her laughter, he nudged slightly closer to her, and his arm brushed against her shoulder.

Adena kept laughing, but she shifted herself slightly too – towards him. Luke tried to ignore the desperate instinct to lean over and kiss those laughing lips, knowing that if he was not careful, he would soon attempt it – and God only knew how Miss Adena Garland would react to her honour's besmirching.

CHAPTER 5

Though the sound of the wave had barely changed, the wind had. The slight breeze that had ruffled his hair when Luke had first encountered this strange and wonderful woman was now a tugging chill, and he could not help but shiver slightly in its wake.

"You are cold," came the gentle voice beside him.

Luke did not think it was worth arguing with: his coat and waistcoat were currently their blankets on the sand and his linen shirt, though expensive, was not designed for outdoor living, and he nodded briefly. "It will pass."

He tried not to catch Adena's eye, but it was just not possible – that smile was bewitching, and even if he had wanted to stay away from it, he could not.

He tilted his head, and caught her knowing look, the twist of her lip as she smiled at him.

"Why do you not say that you are cold because you have given your greatcoat to me?" Adena smiled, and Luke found that the chill of the air was nothing to the heat that she stirred within him.

He shrugged. "You need it more than I, Adena, and I am…I am quite happy to give it to you."

And the words unsaid that soared from his heart whispered, "And I would give you the shirt off my back if you asked me for it."

Perhaps something of the intensity of his thoughts showed on his face, for she blushed, her cheeks mirroring the heat of her hair.

"Maybe," and her voice was even softer now, and her gaze had dropped as her cheeks continued to pink, "we should move a little closer."

Luke swallowed, and when he spoke, his voice was cracked. "To… to the fire?"

It was surely his own imagination. Adena could not be looking at him like that, like she wanted to move closer – as though she felt for him the same startling emotions that were gaining strength in his own chest.

But it was not his imagination when she replied softly, "No, to each other. The fire will only burn us, whereas…well, our shared body heat will keep us warm."

No other woman on this earth had ever said such a thing to Luke, Marquis of Dewsbury, and he had to blink several times to ensure that he was still awake. Was this an invitation to more? He was no stranger to lovemaking – no titled gentleman usually was – but this situation was, of course, unique.

"If you do not want to, I quite understand," she said hurriedly, that flush that was becoming so familiar to him covering her cheeks.

Luke swallowed. If he was not careful, he would regret this for the rest of his life.

"I would be honoured," he said in a low voice.

And then a smile, dazzling in its brilliance as the light of the fire glinted on her lips. Luke tried to calm the natural stirring in his loins. If she wanted more, she would have to ask for it, he reminded himself. He was no seducer of virtue.

Without saying another word, Adena moved closer to him, her arm touching his, her skirted legs sitting alongside his in britches.

Luke felt his breath quickening, and tried to slow his own heartbeat. This was ridiculous. He had had more flirtatious experiences with young women before: gently leaning down to reveal a healthy view of their breasts, the accidental on purpose wetting of the skirts to cling to ankles, the almost casual brush of a hand against a bottom – but this?

He could sense her own breathing as her arm moved closer and then slightly away from his own, but he could not tell whether she was making him warmer, or if his consciousness of her body was doing that for him.

"Better?" Adena whispered, tilting her head slightly to gaze into his eyes.

Luke almost choked down his words that it would be better if they were naked – his first instinct – and instead muttered, "Much better, thank you."

She smiled, and turned her head back to the fire, but he did not take his eyes from her. At first her face, beautiful as it was, but then the soft curves below it, and the gentle swell of her hips that were even now touching him. She was just so soft, so warm, so inviting: and she could not be more different from his own raw hard strength.

"Who could believe this of a marquis?" Adena said lightly with a knowing smile, but without taking her eyes away from the fire. "I think most of the ladies of the *ton* would be absolutely outraged at such behaviour."

Luke could not help but laugh. "Yes, though I am sad to say that it would be you to lose your reputation before I did mine."

She shrugged, and he shivered to feel that shrug as well as see it. "'Tis the way of the world, I suppose. I am not sure if it is even possible to fight against it, though I suppose I am, in my own small way."

The smile on her face faltered, and Luke longed to ask her about her strange comment, but before he could, Adena had tilted her head back and shook her long red hair loose.

"My, but you can never see the stars like this in London."

Luke tilted his head and looked up. Where there was often just glare or smog in the town, here above the wide and open ocean there was nothing but starlight.

"There is Orion, bright and early in the night sky," Adena murmured, almost too low for Luke to hear her. "And there are the Seven Sisters, though you cannot see all of them tonight, Pleione is hiding."

"I would not have guessed that you knew the stars," Luke said quietly, watching her. "But then, perhaps I should no longer be surprised at you, Miss Adena Garland."

A broad smile crept across her face. "And you are unlike any gentleman that I have ever met – and most unlike the only other marquis I have been introduced to, though to be fair he must have been at least three times your age, and so unlikely to entertain in quite the same way."

Luke chuckled. "If you mean the Marquis of Chester, then I could not agree more. See now, there is Pollux."

He raised his arm to point it out, and felt her nuzzle closer to him, and the instinct to clasp her to him had to be fought down.

"I think Pollux is my favourite star," Adena mused.

"There cannot be many young ladies that have a favourite star." Luke had not intended to speak aloud, but the words were out before he could recall them to his tongue.

She glanced at him, and shook her head slightly. "I know, what a disappointment I am! To think that I could have been as empty headed as the rest of them, and here I am, gutting fish, starting fires, and getting into mischief by getting accidentally marooned with a marquis!"

Luke battled down the feeling to place his arm around her, and instead replied, "You are truly unlike any woman I have ever met – but I am glad of it. I like you, Adena."

Immediately, he cursed himself silently. I like you, Adena? What kind of a thing was that to say? Here he was, a man who had prided himself on not getting caught by any of the dangling hooks laid out by the eligible young ladies of the world, and he was throwing himself at this one!

"Well, I always preferred reading to balls," Adena said nonchalantly, either not noticing or choosing not to notice his last sentence. "Though I suppose soon, I will no longer have to go to them at all."

A darkness fell across Luke's heart. Ah, yes. The intended fiancé. For almost an hour, he had managed to forget that she was to be married – that would certainly prevent her from needing to attend balls. After all, what was a ball but a sort of cattle market for women?

My, but he would love to hunt her: to possess her, to make her his own, to ruin her for any other man because he gave her such pleasure that no one else could compare.

And then Luke blinked, and shook his head as though to shake away those thoughts. What was he, some sort of beagle hunting a fox? Her hair may bear the animal's colouring, but she was no prey to be pursued, but a prize waiting to be won.

"It will be a relief to you, I suppose, to be free of such events?"

Adena nodded. "I tell you now, there is nothing more wearisome than a ball in which one is thrust continuously into society that one would rather avoid. I know the people that I like, and those are the only company I would like to keep."

Another spark of jealousy rose within him as Luke tried to imagine the suitor who had won the heart of this incredible woman. He would be intelligent, of course, far more intelligent than he was; titled she had already said, and so wealthy presumably. A strange spectre of a faceless but well-dressed man rose up in Luke's mind, and he hated him.

He could ask; and if he knew Adena, she would

tell him. But he wouldn't. It was far easier to hate the poor man as a nameless soul.

Feeling his arm getting stiff, Luke moved his hand back to lean and stretch it out – and before he could say a word, Adena had unconsciously leaned into his side, and rested her head on his shoulder.

Every part of him was now tingling, all too aware of her closeness, desperate to cling her to him, but aware that the beautiful Adena was acting on instinct at this moment, not thought.

He could kiss her. Those red lips were just inches away, but he wouldn't. Why, he could not tell.

"I must say, it is all rather strange," he said a little stiffly, "how all of our generation are starting to pair off."

Adena looked up at him, completely open to him, completely vulnerable. "Pair off?"

Luke nodded. "You know: getting engaged to be married, and then actually going through with it!"

She chuckled, and he felt the swell of her breasts against his chest. "Well, that is rather the point of an engagement, is it not?"

"I suppose it is," Luke murmured, hoping that he was successfully keeping the bitterness out of his voice, but unsure as to whether or not he was managing it. "Each time that I think a friend is safe, they go and get married. Caershire was the most disappointing; I thought I was safe with him."

"But is it so strange, really," came the soft reply. "We all of us get to an age where we start to…well, feel the desire to find a person to share our time on this earth with. When you come across someone who is not repellent, and mildly interests you, why not 'go and get married' in your words?"

Luke shook his head. "Is that enough? To just find someone who you can tolerate, who you think you will not be bored of in five, or fifty years' time?"

There was a moment of quiet between them, and then Luke felt Adena sigh.

"Sometimes," she said quietly, "that is all you can hope for."

"But there is more – or at least, there should be," countered Luke, nudging a log closer to the fire to watch the sparks fly. "That is what I hope for my friends when they enchain themselves into the married state."

She laughed at this, and nudged him playfully. Luke felt his loins stirring once more. "Enchained?"

"Do you have a better description for it?"

Adena was smiling, and he could see her lips crease out of the corner of his eye. "I would hope that they find a deep happiness with their spouses, all your friends."

Luke knew that the bitterness was going to surface now, but there was nothing that he could do to prevent it. "Ah, deep happiness. Were we not happy, as friends? But that focus, that time and energy, it all moves from our friendship to the marriage, and before you know it, you have not seen them for months – years!"

Adena's hands had been clasped in her lap, but now she moved one of them to rest gently on his thigh, and Luke's heart felt as though it was going to explode. If he had ever needed proof that he was possessed of self-control, even a small amount, it was this.

"Luke, one day you will find someone that you yourself fall in love with – yes, even you," she added, as though she was ready to counter all of his arguments to the contrary. "You will find that person utterly irresistible, and you will find yourself willing to do anything, go anywhere, or lose any friendship in order to have them."

Luke could barely concentrate on her words, so irritated was he with her sentiment. So, that was what this man made her feel, was it? No wonder she was so at ease with him; her future concerns were met, she need never worry again.

"I was not going to say this," he said suddenly, and he felt Adena stiffen by his side, "but I think I have to. By God, Adena, I am a little jealous of this man who you are to marry."

CHAPTER 6

*A*dena started, and was surprised to find herself so closely nestled to the strong man whom she had only met a few hours ago – and who now admitted himself jealous of the man she was to marry?

"I am sure I should not say such a thing," he was continuing, and Adena tried to listen to him whilst controlling the heat of confusion that was rising in her chest as she became more conscious of their closeness – and his bizarre words. "But then I do not want to hold back with you. I feel like…like I can say anything. Even if it means revealing just how envious I am that this man, whoever he is, will have you to himself."

Adena felt the heat rising to her cheeks, and a

twist of fluttering flattery fanned her heart. Why, to think that Luke was jealous, jealous of a man that simply did not exist! Where had he got this idea from, that she was to be married – and should she tell him?

Her hand, before so unconsciously touching his thigh, now seemed like a wanton movement, but Adena did not want to move it. Her hand felt natural there, as though it belonged there.

Luke had turned his head slightly, and he was staring at her now. "Say something," he said in a low tone, his eyes earnestly seeking hers out.

She opened her mouth, but hesitated. Surely it would be wrong to allow him to think that she was engaged to be married when she was not – and a part of her, and it was a growing part of her, wanted him to know that she was not. That she was free. That she could be proposed to.

The thought of him saying such delicious words to her caused another blush, and Adena said distractedly, "Luke, I am confused."

And now it was his turn to be embarrassed. She watched as his forehead crinkled and he fought the instinct to look away, but he swallowed and continued gazing into her eyes as he said, in a low and fervent tone, "Only this. That whoever he is, the man whom you have given your heart to, he is a fortunate man, blessed beyond many, and I would gladly give up the title, or the wealth, to exchange places with him."

Such words, such feeling: Adena's breath caught in her lungs and she found herself leaning closer to him, revelling in the feeling of him.

There was only one thing to say.

"Luke, I am not engaged," she said softly, gazing up at him through her lashes.

If she had expected a jubilant response, she was to be disappointed.

"Not – not engaged?" Luke's frown became more furrowed, and he shook his head slowly as he looked out to the sea again. "Now I am the one who is confused."

Adena smiled at his obvious disquiet, and murmured, "I never intimated that I was engaged to be married, or I should have understood your words – "

"But – you said," Luke interrupted, looking at her once more. "And I cannot quote it exactly, my memory is not exact, but something along the lines that you had started to weary of dukes and titles, and that you were here hiding from your very own future title! Adena, I could not have been mistaken,"

Understanding finally dawned, and a warm shiver moved up her spine as his lips sounded her name.

Adena could not help but laugh. "Oh, Luke, did the word 'hiding' not give you any clue? It is true, a match has been suggested between myself and a certain gentleman – a gentleman who shall remain nameless, so there is no use in asking me – but that match has not been agreed."

Her green eyes watched his dark ones as he began to understand. "So you…you have not accepted…"

"'Tis my parents match, not my choice," she replied quietly. "It would certainly be advantageous for the family, which is why it is pushed so strongly, and has been for these last two years. He is wealthy, to be sure, as we are, but also titled, connected, respected. Everything that my family is not."

Most of the bitterness from her heart was removed before her words reached her mouth, but Adena was not entirely successful, and Luke seemed to notice.

"You tire of him."

"I tire of the whole debacle," Adena sighed, and

she felt Luke's arm move from propping him up to clasp her to his side, his arm hot against her back, his hand by her hip, his fingers delicately placed, and then firmly embracing her curve. A warm glow started between her legs, and she did not understand, and so she kept speaking. "It is unbelievably irritating, to feel the pressure of another's wishes boring down on you for months upon months."

He was watching her. "Your parents wish it?"

Adena tried not to laugh. "I honestly believe that they have wished me to marry for quite some time. My brothers can join the family business, of course, but as a daughter, I am nothing but an expense 'til I am wed. My father is in trade, and the opportunity to marry beyond our class… always attempting to push me onto noblemen, considering every social occasion a mere excuse to meet with a man you cannot like and do not respect…"

"You – you do not like him?"

It was impossible for Adena to be oblivious of the feeling in Luke's words, but she attempted to ignore them – there was no point in her hoping, he was a marquis and undoubtedly had far better prospects back in good society.

But then why the jealousy? Adena glanced at

him, and saw something deep in his eyes that could be…

"I do not like him," she agreed quietly.

Luke smiled at her wryly. "Why?"

Adena opened her mouth, but then closed it again.

"You must have a reason," Luke continued, and she felt the delightful pressure of his fingers on her hip, close to where the mounting heat was pooling in her body. "Everyone has a reason for liking some people and not others."

She turned her gaze to the fire, as the less intense of the two, and tried to laugh nonchalantly. "I suppose it is because there is no connection between us."

There was a moment of silence, broken by just two words from her handsome companion. "No connection."

Adena could not help it; she tilted her face towards him, and saw such an intensity in Luke's face that she almost gasped aloud. "No," she managed. "No connection."

"What does that even mean?" He whispered.

She swallowed, and then replied softly, "I am not attracted to him."

Luke did nothing but gaze into her eyes, but

Adena would have sworn that his grip on her hips, wonderful as it was, tightened and moved lower to cup the roundness of her bottom. Her heart was beating faster, and she knew exactly what she wanted to do, but she knew she would never have the courage.

"I believe that it is important," she found herself saying, in a stronger voice this time, but still breathless, "to feel attracted to one's spouse. After all, how can...can you make love with someone who does not inspire that in you? And...and I do not feel that with him."

They were as close together as Adena thought they could be, but she was wrong. Luke moved his face an inch closer to hers, and his eyes flickered down from her eyes to her lips, wet from speech, partly open with the desire that Adena knew she felt.

"And do you feel it with me?"

Adena almost cried out then, the intensity of the longing was too great, but she stopped herself. She knew exactly what Luke, Marquis of Dewsbury wanted: perhaps she had always known, from the minute that she had laid eyes on him – or he on her. And she wanted it; wanted to be close to him, as close as you could be to a man, and Luke was the one to possess her, to please her, to propose to her, even.

Just one word. That is all it would take for her to say, and she knew that the self-restraint, if self-restraint you could call it, would completely fall away – from both of them.

"Yes," Adena whispered, her eyes sparkling with the desire she could no longer hide and her mouth ready for his kiss. "Yes, I feel it with you, Luke."

She saw a gleam of joy, of triumph, of glory in his eyes, and he bent his head to lower his lips to hers, and hers were open and ready for him, ready for the kiss that would start something so sweet.

And then he paused. They could not be closer, his nose alongside hers, his free hand now tangled in her hair, and he was breathing heavily, and so was she, and yet it had all stopped. So close as they were to succumbing to the pleasure that they knew they both wanted, everything had come to a standstill.

"Luke?" She managed to breath. "Luke, kiss me. Make love to me."

And with a moan that was almost a growl, he did.

EVERY WANT, every thought, every desire: they were all now realised, and Luke had to remind himself to restrain his passions at first, not to overwhelm the beautiful woman that had allowed him to kiss her, to touch her, to claim every delight of her body.

But restraint did not seem to be something that Miss Adena Garland was interested in. The moment that their lips touched, Luke could sense the barely controlled desire in her, and his spirit responded in kind, drawing open her lips like a shell hiding a pearl, and groaning into her mouth at the sweetness of her kiss.

Her hair was so soft, and its fiery red colour contrasted wildly with the golden yellow sand as Luke gently lowered her down, still worshipping her mouth with his own. The hand that was on her hip had enjoyed such sensations already, but now that she was beneath him, and he was encircled in her legs, the same hand held her tight to prevent the instinctive rocking that overwhelmed her.

"Not yet," he managed to say, dragging his lips from hers to look down on her wild and untamed eyes.

Her hands were around his neck, and she pulled him down again, desperate for his kiss – and he was more than willing to give it. She was evidently new to this, utterly untouched, and Luke revelled in the teaching: first slow, then light, then fast and deep as his tongue claimed her completely and she moaned in his mouth.

He was hard now, harder than he had ever felt, but he knew that this was to be a slow lovemaking; her first, and his first that meant anything.

"Oh, Adena," he could not help but murmur as he nuzzled her neck.

This was paradise, alone as they were on this stretch of beach with no one to disturb them, no one to judge them, no one to tell them that they could not glorify in the sweetness of their emotions.

For Luke knew now, if he had not known before. He loved this woman, loved her in a way that shocked and confused him. If he had been told that love at first sight had been real, he would have scoffed – but not now.

Now the feelings of desperate longing and loving passion were tightening within him, and there was nothing more that he wanted to do than bury himself in her and lose himself in the ecstasy he knew was waiting for them.

But not yet. First, he had to make sure that she was enjoying every element of their bodies, and he knew just how.

"Adena," he panted, drawing himself up on his elbow and staring into those startling green eyes. "Do you trust me?"

She stared at him for a moment, as though so lost in the heat rushing through her body that she could not hear him. And then she smiled a lazy smile of lust and want. "Of course, Luke."

He kissed her gently, one hand caressing her cheek, and the other returning once more to that delicious hip – but then he jumped up, pulling her up with him.

"Luke, what are you – "

"Trust me," he said with a smile, and she answered him with one of her own. "Now, close your eyes."

It had been what he had wanted to do the moment that he had seen her, and now he was going to do it. After delving once more into those delicious lips, Luke slowly walked around her, and found it: the ribbons keeping that gown on her body.

Not for long. After checking that her eyes were completely closed, Luke drew back the mane of red hair and swept it across one shoulder, revealing her neck which he kissed lightly as he slowly undid the ribbon.

"Luke, what are you – "

"Trust me," he repeated, and then the bodice of her dress was undone, and he had pulled it down, and Adena gasped to find herself in nothing but her underclothes which Luke soon removed.

And then he had done it. There she was, standing in the moonlight, firelight, and starlight, absolutely naked.

Luke almost came just looking at her, so exquisite was her form. Long legs topped by the most delightful bottom he had ever seen, curved hips with a delicate waist, and as he stepped around her: the glories of glories, that face, that beautiful face with lips open in surprise but eyes closed, breasts swollen with desire and with nipples budding for his touch.

His own Adena. His, and no one else's. He would be the first and last to see this splendid sight. For there was no doubt in Luke's mind that he was going to marry this goddess, this nymph of the sea, this mermaid that seemingly strode out of the ocean and into his heart.

But enough of looking. His fingers had been tingling, desperate to touch, and now was the time. He strode behind her, pulled off his own shirt, and closed the distance between her skin and his own.

Adena cried out in surprise at the heat of his chest, warm from passion, and then she gasped as one of his hands was placed on her hip and the other on her breast.

It was a gasp that turned into a cry of joy as his lips kissed her neck and his hand caressed her nipple, sparking waves of pleasure across her body. Her back arched, pushing into his hand, but he pulled her hip back and made her suffer the squirming pleasure of restraint.

"Oh, Luke – oh, God!"

It was enough to make him turn her around and enter her, but Luke knew that he had to be controlled: she must receive her own pleasure before he took his own, or she would not be ready for him.

His right hand lowered from her breast and there was a moan of disappointment from her that stiffened him even more, but his left moved from her hip to her other breast and she was not to be disappointed for long.

Even from behind her, he saw her eyes flash wide open as he kissed her cheek and slid one of his fingers into that warm place between her legs.

"Adena," he breathed unable to help himself tightening all over as he felt how wet she was.

"What is this – Luke?" Adena breathed in confusion as pleasure danced across her body, and then the answer came in his gentle stroking.

"You are so beautiful," he murmured in her ear as one hand tightened over her breast, playing with her nipple to increase the heat within her, and the other hand gently stroked that part of her that was just ready to explode with sensual pleasure. "There is no one like you, Adena, no one – and I have wanted you, to kiss you, to pleasure you, to bring you to ecstasy, to know you intimately, because you are the most impossible and wonderful woman in the world."

Oh, it was agony to feel her secret place tighten around his finger as he brought her closer and closer to the precipice of agony, but he knew he had to be slow, he knew that only this way would she know complete and utter pleasure – and it could not be too far off.

"Luke – oh God, don't stop!" Adena arched her back and her legs tightened together around his hand and he sped up, increasing the pace of both hands until she screamed his name and it was glorious and unforgettable and she sagged in his arm as she climaxed and he held her gently as the waves of her passion washed over her.

"Oh, Adena," he breathed into her neck. He may have ruined her for any other man, but she had just as surely ruined him for any other woman. How could he share anything like this with another, now that he had felt it with her?

She turned in his arms, and stared at him, wild eyed, almost drunk with the after effects of her sensuous moment, and she smiled at him.

"You – you are the most…the most incredible – "

"We are not finished yet," Luke interrupted with a smile. He leaned down and spread out his greatcoat. "Lie down."

She almost dropped to the ground, so weak were her legs after he had pleasured her, and Luke almost fell over in his haste to remove his britches.

Once again, her eyes widened, but this time it was at the sight of him.

"Luke…" She began, but he was already above her, already kissing her mouth.

"Trust me," he murmured as he broke away and looked her in the eye.

He saw a little nervousness there, but complete faith in him. She nodded.

Luke almost cried out as he nestled between her legs, warm and wet and welcoming, and the feeling of her breasts on his chest was enough to turn any man wild. They kissed as though they would never kiss again, as though they were the only two humans in the world, as though they were drowning and the only thing that could save them was their own mutual desire to explore every pleasure.

His hands seemed to have a life of their own, firstly at her hips, then cupping her bottom towards him and groaning at the temptation to plunge into her at this moment, then caress her breasts, and then her face, and still she kissed him, full of fervent love, and Luke knew that the feelings in his heart were felt by Adena too.

At last there was nothing he could do to stop himself. Pulling himself up, he gazed into Adena's eyes, and smiled at her.

"Look at me," he commanded, and she obeyed willingly, lips apart, wet from his kiss, eyes glazed with the decadence. Luke did not look away, holding her gaze as he carefully tilted her hips up and legs out, and slowly pushed into her.

It was all he could do from shouting out her name as he felt the tightness and wetness of her, saw the shock and surprise in her eyes but then the instant buzz of gratification as she opened up to him, welcoming him, inviting him deeper.

"Luke, I want you," she moaned quietly, her hands grasping at his chest, trying to pull him closer. "Luke, I want you, I need you – oh!"

He had pulled back and thrust in, deeper this time, and he knew that soon, very soon, he would lose all control.

"Adena – Adena!" Luke smiled at her as he finally got her attention, so preoccupied was she with the indulgent warmth of herself around him. "Adena, you have to tell me if you want me to stop, or slow down, you understand?"

She nodded but how could she understand? Luke grinned as he moved his hips from side to side, and she gasped at the sensation of him inside her. She would understand soon enough.

Slowly, slowly to ensure that it was pleasure and not pain that made her cry out, Luke began his rhythm. Though one elbow was propping him, the other hand was free, and it returned to what it did best: drawing out unimaginable pleasure from her breasts.

Adena's eyes had widened as he began moving slowly in and out of her, but they closed in pure delight as the heat in her secret place began to move as waves from the sparking pleasure from her breasts.

"Oh, Luke, yes!"

Luke felt her hips start to move against him, moving in time with his own pace, and he glorified in the way she was losing herself in the moment, losing herself in their lovemaking, losing herself to him and surrendering.

He wanted to kiss her but he wanted to see her face as they grew closer and closer to the peak of their bodies, and so he kissed her, his tongue possessing her own, and then as he felt himself near the end he pulled away, and looked into her eyes.

They were open. They had captured his the moment he had seen her on the beach and they captured him now as he ploughed into her and twisted her nipple between his fingers and he came, pouring himself into her with rapid movement and he heard her cry out his name and he called out hers, and it was everything, and it was life and love, and he wanted to make love to her every day of his life.

CHAPTER 7

*T*his was the worst pillow that Luke had ever slept on, and the starching was so poor that he even opened his eyes to stare at it in disgust – and discovered that his greatcoat had slipped out from under his cheek. He was lying directly on the sand.

And he was naked, covered by his large greatcoat. And he was not alone.

Without moving so as to not disturb the beautiful and equally naked woman beside him, Luke stared at the waves of red hair that covered her back, and all of his memories from the evening before came flooding back.

Adena. The beach – the island. The fire. The fish. Their passion.

A broad smile broke out on his face as he recalled the intensity of their lovemaking, and his eyes took in the gentle curve of her bottom and the way her flaming hair was peppered with sand.

He could never have believed it if he had woken up alone; would have considered her a fairy, or a mermaid perhaps, gone in the morning light after a night of passion.

And yet here she was. Completely nude, as was he, for they had fallen asleep within minutes of claiming that forbidden treasure from each other, and now it was morning, and –

Luke's eyes widened. It was morning. The beach would be connected to the mainland now, and that meant that anyone could come here. Anyone could walk over the sandy shore and find two completely naked people, and it would not take much guesswork to comprehend what they had been up to.

He scanned the horizon, and his tense body relaxed slightly. The sun was only just coming up. The tide would still be moving, and none but the fishermen of Marshurst would be awake this early.

They had time. Not much, but enough.

"Good morning."

Luke started, and twisted onto his side to stare

into the most beautiful face he had ever seen – would he ever grow used to it?

"Good morning," he murmured, smiling at Adena. "Did you sleep well?"

She returned his smile sleepily, her eyes slightly glazed as she rose back to conscious, and then that consciousness told her in no uncertain terms that she was completely naked.

Her mouth dropped open, and she tilted her body slightly so that it was hidden from his eyes.

"My – my clothes!" She spluttered.

Luke's smile broadened, but he did not tease her. Who knew what sort of temper his future wife really possessed, with hair that colour?

"They are just over there," he said, glancing over his shoulder to show her where. "And do not concern yourself, there is no one here but ourselves. We are still quite alone."

The furrow of Adena's brow disappeared, and a relaxed smile pinched her cheeks. "Well, that is a relief," she said with a sigh. "I thought for a moment that we would be spotted, and forced to explain ourselves! That would have been an…interesting conversation."

Luke returned her smile, but not as broadly. There was a sense of shame in her features, or embarrassment, he could not tell which. Perhaps she regretted what they had done – what they had felt, what they had experienced together?

But no, it was surely more simple than that. She had never been so exposed before, he had been able to tell the moment that they had kissed that she had never been with another man before. It was this vulnerability, this nakedness which disconcerted her, to be sure.

"Last night," he began, but he was interrupted.

"Nevertheless, I should dress," Adena said, and she rose by turning away from him, leaving him with just the sight of those long legs and her sweeping red hair. "Anyone could be along now, I suppose?"

Luke rolled onto his back, and shrugged. "I suppose so, but – "

"And your clothes are here too, would you like them?"

He stared up at her, already halfway into her undergarments. "'Tis a pity to hide that beauty so quickly."

She blushed, but it was not the same as last night. This truly was embarrassment rather than pleasure at the compliment.

"Last night," Luke persevered, "I just wanted to say – "

"You do not need to say a word," Adena said shortly, fumbling with her gown as she attempted to turn it the right way out and remove as much sand from it as possible. "I would think that the least said about it, the better. Do not you?"

Luke swallowed, and sat up, vaguely conscious now that he was still naked and she was almost dressed. "No," he said simply.

Her head turned and she stared at him. "No?"

He shook his head, and rose. "Adena, I would like to see you again after we return to the mainland. Meet your family."

There was a strange look in her eye, one that he could not decipher. She was evidently fascinated by his nude body, but felt unable to look at him. Her eyes kept glancing off it as though it was oil and she was water.

"And why," she replied slowly, "would you want to do that?"

Luke laughed, and shook his head. "Well, is it not obvious? I wish to know you better."

Adena caught his eye now, staring at him in an almost accusing manner. "Get to know me better?"

Luke swallowed. He wanted to marry her, he

knew that, and she must do too – how could she not, after what they had shared? But he knew the rules of decorum, and it was evident that she did too. He would need to ask her father first, before he got down on one knee, and asked her the most important question of his life.

"Yes, get to know you better," he said with a smile, and a look full of love and meaning so that she could understand him. "I would like to meet your father, and your mother. Be introduced to them, and make their acquaintance."

She was looking at him as though he was mad, and being away from her was painful. All Luke wanted to do was sweep her into his arms and kiss her, kiss her like he had done last night. You never know, perhaps they could both enjoy a repeat performance before they returned to civilisation.

Adena must have read something of his thoughts in his expression, for she said hurriedly, "I do not think that is a good idea, my lord, and – "

"My lord?" Luke took a step towards her – until Adena took a step back.

He stopped dead. "I am not going to hurt you."

"I know that," Adena replied hurriedly, seemingly unable – or unwilling – to look him in the eye. "It is just…I need to find my shawl. I think I left it further down the beach. I will return shortly."

Without another word, she was striding down the beach, sand flowing from her steps in the light breeze, and hair billowing behind her.

Luke stared open mouthed. It was incomprehensible: to think that they had bared their souls to each other just hours before. He had revealed his tragic family history, she had told him about her arranged marriage, for want of a better word. They had made love, and she had enjoyed it, there was no possibility that he had misunderstood that.

So what had happened? Had sleep reversed the feelings that she had experienced that evening? Had the rules of society returned to her, and she had felt the impropriety of what they had shared?

Luke shook his head, and reached for his britches. Miss Adena Garland may be able to act with nonchalance after a night of lovemaking but it was not in his spirit to allow the woman he loved to simply wander off without him. She could not have made it more clear that she simply wanted to draw a line under the sand, and forget about it.

Well, if that is what she wanted, he was far too much of a gentleman to give her any concern. Perhaps she would go back to London, Luke thought savagely, and marry that man after all. She would need assurances, he supposed, to ensure that the news would never reach this man, or her family, or society at large.

He would tell her. He would find her, and tell her that their secret would be safe with him.

But first, he really should get dressed.

ADENA BRUSHED ASIDE the tears that were threatening to form in her eyes, and kept on walking. She would not look back. She would not give that marquis the satisfaction of knowing just how much he had hurt her.

How could he say those things to her? That he wanted to get to know her parents, without any sign, without any words of love or affection – or marriage? It was all very well to make their acquaintance, but plenty of gentleman had done so, and none but two had ever led to proposals of marriage. Her beauty had not been enough to conquer most of their disapproval at her father's wealth from trade.

"Do not be ridiculous, Adena," she told herself

aloud, under her breath. "Marriage, what were you thinking?"

Memories from the previous night burned into her thoughts as her eyes looked around for the lost shawl. That was what she was thinking – and she could not stop thinking about it. To discover that there was such passion, such delight to be found in the body of another!

She had shared herself with him willingly, there was no doubt of that. Adena's cheeks crimsoned to think of the wanton way that she had given herself to a man she had only just met, but was there not a meeting of minds? Had he not seemed to be the perfect man: strong yet thoughtful, practical and considerate, and oh, so handsome!

"You are a fool," she muttered. "After all this time of attempting to hide from that stupid man, to avoid marriage, you really thought that after meeting a man for a few hours that marriage would be on the cards?"

But she had thought it. Fool she may have been, but it was a foolishness borne from romanticism, not idiocy. As her feet were kissed by the disappearing tide, Adena remembered with a smile the words that Luke had said to her.

"There is no one like you, Adena, no one – and I have

wanted you, to kiss you, to pleasure you, to bring you to ecstasy, to know you intimately, because you are the most impossible and wonderful woman in the world."

But it had not been enough. When she had awoken that morning, what words of love had he spoken? What proposal of marriage had he made? Nothing, none, no words at all.

"You could have said something yourself, but no," Adena chastised herself, slowing her pace down now and twisting a lock of her hair around her fingers. "Far be it for you to presume on marriage."

And yet…

Her imagination could not be tamed. She saw herself his wife, his bride, walking down the altar to meet him, welcoming friends into their home, ascending the stairs at night to return to their bed, and their passions, and their ecstasy…

"Ridiculous," she said firmly, perhaps a little louder than she had been expecting. "If he had wanted to marry you, Adena, he would have asked you immediately. He would have known what honour had demanded, or he would have felt the desire to claim me, or…"

Or else, and these words were far too painful to say aloud, or else he simply did not wish to marry you. There you were, a woman on an island for the night, easy to seduce. You even told him that you were attracted to him, that you wanted him. You allowed him to kiss you, to undress you, to −

And here even her words gave out, and a deep blush moved across her cheeks. It had been wicked, but it had been wonderful.

Irritated with the lack of shawl and tired of striding along a beach with seemingly no end, Adena threw herself onto the sand and stared at the ocean.

Less than a day ago she was enjoying almost an identical walk along the beach. How much had changed since then!

"Adena?"

Startled, she jumped, and turned to see Luke emerging from behind a tree, holding her shawl.

"I found this under…under my greatcoat," he said with an easy smile, and her insides squirmed to see him.

Why, she could not even be angry at him for not loving her. How could she? He was such an incredible man, and had suffered so much already. Perhaps it was easier for him never to love again, to never feel loss again.

And then a fiery spike of anger rose in her

heart. Why was she making excuses for him? No one forced him to return her shawl, at any rate.

"Thank you," she said stiffly. "I had wondered where it had got to."

She did not beckon him closer, or invite him to sit down beside her, and yet he did both.

Smiling, he nudged her with his shoulder. "I hope you are not too hungry, but I am not sure whether any fish that I could catch or cook would be much help to you."

Adena could not tell whether she was seething with anger, or boiling over with hurt. She nodded, and kept her eyes out to sea.

Luke seemed to be hesitating, but eventually he said in a low voice, "It should not be necessary for me to say this but…I wish to say it anyway. You do not even have to ask me to keep what happened between us last night…well, between us. No one else ever need know."

Bitter tears sprung up in Adena's eyes, but she blinked them away. So, he wanted to keep it an utter secret? It would certainly prevent him from needing to marry her. Why did she love this man if all he wanted to do was hurt her, leave her?

Not trusting her voice, she nodded.

"I did not know whether you needed…assurance," he continued almost in a whisper, as though they were surrounded by others who may wish to listen in to their conversation. "So I wanted you to know that no word of this will ever escape my lips. It will…it will be as though nothing ever happened."

Not for me, Adena wanted to cry. How do you think that I can ever go back to normal life again, knowing you as I do, knowing that you will be out there, somewhere in the world, charming the next woman whom you encounter? How can I return to my old life, without the innocence that you took from me? Knowing what pleasure we shared?

"That is very kind of you," she replied stiffly, forcing down the flood of emotions and not taking her eyes away from the sea. "I imagine that if we ever meet in town, we can do so as indifferent acquaintances."

For a moment, he did not say anything. Adena barely dared to breathe: was this it? Was this the moment that he declared himself?

"I will follow your lead of course, Miss Garland." Luke spoke stiffly, and it drove a dagger into her heart. "If you wish to pretend that we have never even met, I shall oblige."

CHAPTER 8

*A*dena swallowed. Everything that she had hoped would not come to pass was now a reality.

He did not love her. He did not even seem to like her, he seemed so willing, so happy to never see her again or claim their friendship.

It had all evidently been in her head. What she thought they had shared was just an illusion, a hope, a fantasy.

Now that she had come crashing down to earth, it was not a pleasant experience.

"The tide is almost out," she said dully.

Her shawl was placed in her lap, and she looked down at it through misty eyes.

"So it is," said Luke stiffly. "We should be able

to get over to the mainland soon. We could wait here for a few more minutes, and then – "

"No," Adena said resolutely. "I would like to start now."

The last thing that she wanted was to spend an extra minute with Luke, the Marquis of Dewsbury, if she did not have to. All this time with him was just painful; every time she looked at him, she remembered being in those arms, kissing that mouth.

"Now?" Luke replied blankly.

She did not reply, but instead rose and started to dust down the sand from her gown.

"Now," he muttered quietly under his breath, though she caught it quite easily, and the sarcasm in his voice pulled at her heart. Could he not see the pain she was feeling?

For a moment, as Luke rose too, and brushed some dried seaweed from his linen shirt, Adena felt an overwhelming desire to tell him. Exactly what she would say, she was not quite sure. There had to be some way of telling him that she had fallen painfully and irrevocably in love with him, without him feeling obliged to propose marriage to her.

Because she could not bear the thought of Luke proposing out of a misplaced sense of duty, or honour. She wanted him to want her – passionately, compulsively, as she did him.

But if she shared even a snippet of this, she knew what the outcome would be. He would propose out of respect to custom, and they would marry, and she would have to spend the rest of her life looking over at a husband who had not really wanted to marry her.

No. She would not be that selfish. She could not stand it. She would be silent, and let him return to society, free and unencumbered.

Though she would never be free of the thought of him again.

"'Tis this way."

Luke's voice broke into her thoughts, and she coloured as though he could sense that he was on her mind. He was indicating the direction which she had taken to search for her shawl.

"Off we go then," Adena tried to say without a care in the world, half knowing, half hoping that he would hear the quaver in her tones and enquire whether anything was the matter. All she needed was an opening, an excuse…

"I think you mentioned that you were staying with some friends nearby," Luke asked her formally as they reached the wet sand near the shore and started to walk along it. "Will they be concerned about your welfare?"

Adena sighed. Back to small talk and polite conversation it was, then. It was hard to believe what they had been together for that sparkling night.

"I should think," she replied cordially. "I imagine there may be a small search party looking for me, but I suppose that as it was just one night, they may assume that I took lodgings in Marshurst instead of returning home."

They strode on for a few more minutes in silence as they came around a bend, and the mainland came into clearer view – as did a stretch of beach connecting them to it.

Adena's shoulders sagged with relief. "Ah, there it is!"

Luke laughed quietly. "You were concerned that it would not be?"

"Not at all," she laughed in return, glorifying in their conversation now that it was returning to something that felt like normal. "It was just – now, that is strange."

She stopped and stared down at the sand. Luke came to a stop beside her, and stared down uncomprehending at the same patch of sand.

"What are we looking at?"

Adena leaned down, and brushed at the sand with her fingers. It was dry, moving fluidly across her fingers and pooling in her palm.

"'Tis just sand," said his voice beside her.

She shook her head. "No, it is dry sand. Completely dry. Bone dry."

Her heart was racing. It did not make sense.

"What does that matter?" Luke's voice sounded bored now, and as she stood up, he gave her a relaxed smile. "There is bound to be some dry sand here, the tide never comes up this far."

Something was nagging at the back of her mind, and Adena could not precisely put her finger on it, but it definitely had something to do with the sand.

"The tide never comes up this far," she repeated slowly, rubbing her fingers together to feel the dry grains on her skin.

Luke shook his head, and stared out at the small scattering of houses that they could just about make out on the mainland. "No, it only usually makes it up to that line, you can see clearly where the sand goes from dark to light. That is why this place is used to get back – "

His voice broke off abruptly, and all of a sudden, Adena understood.

"To get back to the mainland," she said quietly, staring at Luke in amazement. But there was no amazement on his face. There was horror.

"Adena," he began, but she spoke over him.

"You knew! You knew that there was a place where the tide did not reach, where the sand was still dry, where you could still get across to the mainland!"

He was staring at her, aghast, and Adena could feel fiery anger bubbling up inside her.

"Listen to me – "

"I will not listen to you!" Adena almost shouted, she was so furious. "You knew that we could have made our way back to shore last night, did you not? You knew that we were not really trapped – Squire's Isle indeed!"

"That is the local name," Luke said hurriedly.

Adena made an irritated sound. "So you gave me the correct name for it, do you believe that this suffices? Did it slip your mind to mention that we could also make our way home last evening, too? Did you accidentally forget that we were not marooned on an island?"

His mouth was opening and closing now but no words were coming out of it.

Adena flung back her head and laughed bitterly. She had been so stupid, so stupid! "Is this a trick that you play on all visiting gentlewomen?"

"Trick – no!" Luke shook his head violently and tried to reach for her hands, but she snatched them away. "Adena, listen. I should have told you that we could have walked, but – "

"Yes, you should!" She did not care for his excuses, did not care that her heart was breaking all over again – to think that she could experience such pain! "Is this just a joke to you? Do you find it funny to lie to innocent young ladies about how they are trapped all night on an island, just with you?"

She started to walk away from him, determined to put as much distance between him and her as possible, but he walked after her, and his strides were longer.

"Adena, listen, I knew that I should tell you but I was so intrigued by you, so fascinated – "

But Adena did not want to hear it. "I have heard enough!"

"You must listen to me!" Luke grabbed her arm and tried to twist her around to face him, but she struggled against him. "Please, you must believe me that I had nothing but good intentions for hiding the truth!"

"Like seducing me?" Adena wrenched at her arm but she could not get herself free, and she was hotly aware of how close he was, how strong he was, how quickly he could fold her in his arms and kiss away all her protestations.

And by God, she would let him.

No! He lied to her, manipulated her, allowed her to let her guard down.

"I had no intention of seducing you," Luke was saying, "quite the opposite!"

She laughed as her arms started to burn with his pressure. "Oh, so now I was not tempting enough for you?"

He stared at her, bewildered. "Which offends you more?"

But his confusion had allowed him to drop his guard, and Adena pulled away her arm, rubbing at it with her other hand.

"Leave me alone," she said firmly. "If I had just continued to walk around this island, or so I thought it was, I would have found my way home. If you had not stopped me, told me that it was impossible, then I would not have stayed here, with you, to…to…"

Tears were returning once more, but she was not going to let them overwhelm her. She found her footing on the sand, and continued to walk back to the mainland.

But Luke was not going to give up that easily, it seemed. Keeping apace beside her, where there was nothing that she could do to prevent him from following her, he continued to plead with her.

"Yes, I was wrong to allow the deception – but it was too perfect, the first moment that I saw you I knew that I wanted to get to know you, to – to befriend you – "

Adena let out a bark of a laugh, dark and sarcastic.

"I mean it!" Luke ran a few paces and stopped directly before her, forcing her to stop. She stared into those grey eyes and tried to quash the rush of love that was rising up in her. "Adena, I was wrong, I admit it. But as soon as I realised how beautiful you were, how funny you are, how spirited you are…it was impossible for me to let you go without trying to charm you, win you to me."

"To take advantage of me!"

"To make you love me!"

Adena was breathing heavily, and her arm still hurt, but it was nothing to the pain that was ebbing slowly into her soul as she stared into the face of a man she had thought was good, and kind.

But he was no such thing.

"You mean to tell me," she said slowly, staring into his eyes and refusing to look away, refusing to let the tears fall. "That you intended to secure my affections? That you acted purposefully to make love to me?"

Luke's shoulders sagged as though in relief, and he smiled. "Yes."

The slap across his face rang out across the water, echoing over the sea in all directions.

"You cad," she said softly. "You have no thoughts for others, only for your own. You do not love me, or anyone, it seems. All you are interested in is yourself. You make me sick."

Picking up her skirts, Adena ran across the sand, tears now finally falling after such resolute control, back to civilisation.

LUKE STARED after her in horror. That had not been what he had meant at all – he had just declared his love in the only way that he knew how, and somehow it had gone all wrong.

How was this even possible? Could he have been more direct? Admittedly, the word love had not yet passed his lips – but he had not been raised to show any emotions. Just the few words that he had been managed had been against his nature.

Perhaps he had needed to bare his soul even further to this mysterious and wonderful woman who had strode into his life through the waves, and now was running away from him across the sand.

Luke's heart ached as he saw the figure grow smaller and smaller into the distance. Well, he had royally messed that up completely. What sort of an idiot was he? To be sure, his friends and even a few brothers had come to him for guidance in these matters, and like an idiot, he had given them his advice.

And yet when it had really mattered, when his own heart was on the line, he had been powerless to prevent it from all falling apart.

Luke kicked at some sand and watched it fly out into the wind. He could berate himself for his choice of words all he wanted, of course, but it all came down to one decision: his choice to lie, and conceal the truth of the island.

What would have happened if he had been

honest in that moment: would she have stayed for a few hours with him? Probably not.

Would she have permitted him to walk her home? Perhaps, but it would have been a walk of an hour, nothing more.

It was entirely possible that, after he had rescued her from the rising tide, she would have just simply thanked him and gone on her way.

Luke bit his lip, and started to walk heavily along the same way that Adena had done. There was no use thinking about it, he supposed. The fact of the matter was that he had already chosen: there was no way of going back and undoing the stupid mistake that he had already made.

And the consequences were severe. All hope of ever seeing Miss Adena Garland again were at an end, he knew that. If chance should bring him into her company, she would not only ignore him, but certainly cut him off, reject him, leave the party, perhaps.

A flash of memory passed through his mind: the feel of her breast under his hand, the sensation of her body writhing against his.

But they were overpowered by the recollection of her laughter, the way she threw her head back to gaze at the stars, her admission that she found him attractive, the curl of her lips as she had laughed at his inept cooking.

Luke swore under his breath. Only he could find his perfect woman, charm her, delight her, strip her down and make love to her under the stars… and then lose her, all in one day.

CHAPTER 9

*A*dena almost collapsed into the large wooden chair that sat in the hallway of the Kerrs, but whether it was from physical or emotional exhaustion, she could not tell.

In a strange way, it was as though she had never left. The grandfather clock was still ticking away, showing that the time was a quarter to nine. The candle near the door was a tad more burned down than she had remembered it, but other than that, the hallway looked exactly as it had done the last time that she had seen it.

She laughed under her breath. It could all have been a dream, for the difference that the last night had made to her life. Here she was, a little sandier than before, and in desperate need of a good wash, but nothing more.

The grandfather clock chimed the quarter hour, and a door opened to the breakfast room.

" – and if no sign of her shows up soon, then we will have to inform – Adena!"

Adena was almost flattened by a rush of golden brown hair and sobs.

"Rowena!"

"Oh, Adena, we thought we had lost you," her friend sobbed, breaking away from her to stare at her wildly. "You did not return from your walk, and I waited up all night! The search party, it could not find you…"

Adena could see the truth of it in her friend's eyes: they were rimmed with grey, and red from tears.

"We thought something terrible had happened to you!" Rowena clutched at her friend's hands, and drew them close to her. "But you are here – and you are alive!"

"Alive?" Adena tried to force a laugh, but it felt and sounded hollow. "My dear Rowena, you must accept my apologies, I must have given you such a fright. Were you concerned?"

"You have been gone all night," Rowena said breathlessly, her eyes wide. "Where have you been?"

Adena swallowed. She should have expected this rather obvious question, and yet she had had no time to construct a believable answer. Thankfully, because she had time to answer, another voice entered the fray.

"My word, it is Miss Garland!" Rowena's father, a tall man with an almost continuous smile the entire time that Adena had known him, was hurrying out of the breakfast room with concern and fear on his visage.

"'Tis indeed, and she is quite safe," Rowena said hastily. "That is – you are not hurt, are you?"

"Fetch a doctor," said Mr Kerr decidedly to a servant who was gawking at the three of them from the breakfast room doorway. "Quickly now!"

Adena could not help but laugh genuinely now, it all seemed so strange after her night on the island – what she had thought was the island. "I am uninjured."

Leaving aside the broken heart of course, her inner voice wanted to speak aloud, but she quashed down that particular thought as Mrs Kerr came through the door, her arms full of flowers she had just picked from the garden – flowers that were strewn on the floor as she jumped at the sight of her daughter's missing friend.

"Lord save us, Miss Garland! You are back!"

"Yes," said Adena helplessly, giving herself up to the chaos. "And I must apologise profusely for giving you such – "

"A doctor," said Mrs Kerr hurriedly, moving over to her and feeling her forehead with the back of her hand. "A doctor must be sent for."

"A doctor has been sent for, Mama," Rowena said with a smile, and Adena was pleased to see that she had relaxed somewhat. Her attention seemed to have moved on, and though her smile was genuine, it was a little more vacant than Adena was accustomed to. "Come now, I will help Miss Garland up to her room."

There were many shouted protestations to this – Miss Garland could not possibly be moved, how could she think of it? Was it not best for them to wait for the doctor to arrive?

But eventually Adena was able to convince them that really, all she wanted was a little peace and quiet to rest from what Mrs Kerr termed as 'her ordeal'.

Exactly what that ordeal consisted of, she would not say, simply affirming her desire for rest.

"Well, if you are quite sure," said Mrs Kerr, unconvinced.

Her husband nodded at his daughter. "Rowena will help you upstairs, and we shall send the doctor up directly."

It was a relief for Adena, after spending so much time with just herself and − another, as she would call him in her mind from now on − to be away from such a crowd of people, as the butler, two more maids, and a footman had all arrived to see what the commotion had all been about.

Finally the bedroom door was closed, and she and Rowena were alone.

"What a noise!" Adena threw herself onto the bed and closed her eyes. "I thought that we would never escape them all!"

For a moment, she thought that Rowena had departed from the room, for there was no reply. She opened her eyes, and saw her friend seated at the dressing table, fiddling with her hairbrush.

"I am glad to be back," said Adena, more quietly now. "It was…a rather strange experience, I must say."

She was not one to attempt to be mysterious on purpose, but she had expected her rather obtuse comment to provoke questions from her friend.

But Rowena did not turn around, did not even catch her gaze in the mirror. "Hmmm?"

Adena propped herself up on the bed, and relaxed into the soft delight of the cushions. "I never thought I would be so glad to be in a bed again!"

That, surely, was enough of a bizarre statement to elicit a response – and perhaps it may have been, for a companion who was not otherwise lost in her own thoughts. Rowena Kerr, however, seemed distracted, unable to concentrate.

"Rowena, I have to tell you," Adena said in a rush. She knew that she would be overcome if she did not tell someone, and as her closest friend, who better to act as her confidante. "I met a gentleman."

This at last seemed to be the cue for Rowena's attention. She started, turned around, and smiled mischievously. "A gentleman, you say! One that I am acquainted with?"

Adena hesitated. Happy as she was to share most of the details of her story, there were some elements – some moments, some experiences – that were better kept to herself. After all, and she blushed to consider it, would she want Luke sharing exactly what they had become to each other with his closest friends?

"I am not sure," she said carefully. "He is a marquis, and not of this neighbourhood."

The interest in Rowena's eyes flickered and died, and her shoulders slumped. "Oh, I suppose not then."

Her gaze slipped away from her friend, and settled onto what appeared to Adena at least as a very uninteresting piece of carpet.

"As I was saying," she continued, rather pertly, "I met him. He is – oh, Rowena, he is unlike any other person that I have ever met, any gentleman for sure."

Rowena sighed. "Handsome?"

"Very," Adena nodded, and a small smile sparked across her lips. "And yet, sometimes you can almost forget that. When you are speaking with him, I mean. His conversation is so captivating, you can at times lose yourself in....Rowena, are you listening?"

Rowena moved with a start, and gazed at Adena wildly. "What?"

Adena stared at her friend, now more curious about her than interested in sharing her story. "What has got into you, Ro? Has anything happened?"

It looked at first like Rowena was going to

speak: her mouth opened and her cheeks flushed at the upcoming words, but then she seemed to decide against it.

"You must be tired," she said quietly, rising from her seat and moving to the door. "I will leave you to rest, and prevent the doctor from being sent up when he arrives."

Without another word, she had left the bedroom. Adena stared after her in confusion. And she had thought that she would possess the more interesting secret.

LUKE'S HAND felt heavy as he knocked on the door of his friend's estate, and waited the expected two or three minutes for the elderly butler to arrive at the door.

"My lord," said the old man in pleasant surprise. "What an honour. I am afraid that Sir Moses – "

"Sir Moses will see me," Luke interrupted, without the typical grace and elegance that he utilised when in society. "I am sorry, Andrews."

Pushing past the elderly gentleman who gently protested at the intrusion, Luke strode into the

Great Hall of Wandorne and made his way to the room where he knew he would find the miser at this hour, or at any hour for that matter.

The library had its shutters still closed, and naught but one solitary candle gave light to the room. Sir Moses was hunched in a chair by the unlit grate.

"Andrews? Is that you?" He said gruffly without looking up.

Luke strode forward, removed the book from his friend's hands, and dropped into the chair opposite. "I am in trouble, Moses."

The long-haired man scowled at him. "Dang it all, Dewsbury, at least put a bookmark in it."

Luke rolled his eyes, grabbed at a letter that was lying on the floor beside his chair, and stuffed it into the book. "I do not know how you can live like this, Moses, 'tis barbaric."

Sir Moses shrugged. "I like it. That is all that matters."

Sighing, Luke placed the book down on the floor. He had heard that Moses had allowed himself to wallow in his unhappiness, but he had not expected anything like this.

"When we left Cambridge," he said sternly to his friend. "You promised me that you would try to get back to living. To put aside the past, and take up your estate's duties once more."

Sir Moses glared at him, and shrugged once more. "I lied."

Luke held his friend's gaze for a few seconds, and then they both laughed.

"Come, ring the bell and we can get some brandy in here," said Sir Moses with a wave of his hand. "Trouble, you say? Not a woman, 'tis never a woman with you. Gambling?"

Luke winced as he leaned over to pull the bell beside the fireplace.

"Hurt your shoulder then – hunting accident?"

"Outdoor sleeping," corrected Luke with a wry smile. "If I tell you that it is a bit of a strange predicament, would you believe me?"

He took the moment when they both laughed again to examine his friend, and he was concerned with what he saw. It had been six months since he had last visited Sir Moses, more of a recluse now than anything else, shut up as he was here in Wandorne. It was almost impossible to believe that they were the same age, give or take a few months.

Bitterness had aged Sir Moses; aged him in body and spirit, and Luke felt nothing but pity to see it.

"A strange predicament? I'll say." Sir Moses broke off as a footman stumbled into the dark room from the bright corridor, placed a bottle of brandy and two glasses – there seemed to be nothing else his friend rang for, Luke thought – and poured out a very large measure into each. "Tell me all about it, I could do with a new story."

Luke took a gulp of the brandy, a large breath, and launched into his story.

It felt strange at first, sharing Adena with another – but then he knew of no other close friend for more than thirty miles, and he knew that if he did not tell someone soon, he would go utterly mad.

He told Sir Moses about the walk, the woman in the water ("My God!") and the temptation to hide the truth ("I knew you would get yourself into a tangle somewhere."). He told him about the fire and the shelter ("You never were one for the outdoors!") and the fish, which generated the biggest laugh that he had seen in Sir Moses for over two years.

But when he came to the end of the evening, he hesitated. He had told her, even though he had not technically promised, that he would not tell a soul about that particular part of their encounter. What sort of a gentleman would he be if he did not keep to his word?

But Sir Moses did not need that part of the story spelled out to him. "Well, I suppose you did what any of us would have done in the circumstances. You sly old dog, why am I not surprised?"

Luke coloured. "It was not like that. Adena – Miss Garland – means a…a great deal to me."

Sir Moses stopped smiling, and leaned forward. "Ah. That type of trouble."

Luke squirmed slightly in his chair. "Normally I am having this conversation the other way around – 'tis other people coming to me with their love woes."

His friend raised an eyebrow. "Hmmm. And what do you normally tell them?"

Luke's gaze moved from his friend, and glanced around the room. There was no better word for it than dilapidated – or perhaps, unloved. If he had not found Sir Moses sitting here, and knew so well of his love for books, then he would have guessed that this room had been uninhabited for months, if not years.

"Luke, you have dug yourself into a hole, but 'tis only an inch deep." Sir Moses' voice recalled his attention, and he saw that his friend was smiling wryly. "Do you not see that you have the easiest answer in the world?"

"No, "replied Luke leaning forward eagerly. "What should I do?"

Sir Moses leaned forward in turn, and lowered his voice to a whisper, as though he was revealing a deep and terrible secret. "Find the girl, and marry her."

A feeling of despair sunk into Luke's stomach. "I cannot do that."

"Why not?" Sir Moses leaned back and raised an eyebrow. "If you have found even a modicum of happiness with this woman, then I advise you to cling onto it for dear life. Do not...do not make the mistake that I did."

A dull look had now surfaced into Sir Moses' eyes, and Luke reached out and gripped his hand. "Moses – "

"Luke," returned his friend fiercely. "You have no reason not to marry her, so why are you here? Why the trouble?"

Luke swallowed. "If she had wanted that, she would have...I mean, she gave no sign that – "

"Did you tell her that you loved her?" Sir Moses interrupted, a sharp look on his face.

Luke opened his mouth, shut it, and shook his head.

"God's teeth man, she is not a mind reader!"

Luke laughed bitterly. "I thought that she would want it done properly, you know, ask her father first and then – "

"You had hardly gone about it properly up until then, why bother now!" Sir Moses exploded, looking quite deranged. "She must have expected you to speak, after you had shared…well, you know. To say nothing after such an encounter was tantamount to a rejection from you!"

Luke's eyes widened. It all seemed so obvious now, now that Moses said it, but at the time he had been so focused on decorum, on propriety.

"I was so concerned about doing the right thing," he said slowly, "that I did the wrong thing."

Sir Moses shook his head, and rose. "You are not the first, and you certainly will not be the last. Come on."

Luke rose in a daze. "Where are we going?"

"Going?" Sir Moses gave a bark of a laugh, and put his arm around his friend as he walked him to the door. "We are going to find this woman of yours, of course."

It had taken over half an hour of persuasion for Adena to receive permission from Mr and Mrs Kerr when she had requested to visit the local town. She could understand their hesitancy for letting her out of their sight after her disappearance three days ago – and they had promised her parents to keep an eye on her. Adena was also irritatingly aware that they had been requested by her parents to encourage her suit with the odious man from London.

She had hoped that Rowena would have been on her side, but she had vaguely suggested that she would be willing to accompany Adena, and that seemed to reassure her parents. Surely Miss Garland could not go missing again if she was with their daughter.

Adena had been thrilled at the idea of getting back to a town, and with Rowena by her side. She had taken her reticule with a few shillings in it, and had hoped that the two of them could peruse the latest bonnets, purchase a few ribbons, and enter their favourite coffee house for the latest news.

But on arriving into town, Rowena had muttered about an errand she must perform, and had wandered swiftly down a side street that Adena did not know. She had paused there, irresolute for almost a full minute, before drawing herself up and deciding to leave her. If Rowena wanted to be alone, she would respect her wishes.

But it simply was not the same when she was on her own. The bonnets were dull, the ribbons over-priced, and far earlier than Adena had expected, she found herself stepping through the door into the most fashionable coffee house in the town, and settling herself down onto a comfortable chair with the latest paper before her.

The aroma of the coffee revived her spirits slightly, and determined to make the trip at least partly worth the effort of driving out here, she placed her order for coffee, sipped it delightedly when it arrived, and picked up the paper.

The Regent was splashed across it, as he always was, though Adena was not really interested to see whether the editor had decided in favour or against his latest antics.

She skipped over the international news too, finding the news of war too depressing for a heart already forlorn, and started to gaze down the adver-tisements.

There was a new way of curling one's hair that looked highly suspicious in her mind, and one company appeared to be underselling fabric at a ridiculous price. Adena pursed her lips. There must be something wrong with it, there was simply no such thing as good quality muslin at that price.

And then her eye was caught by something on the opposite page. For a moment, she could not entirely register what it was that had focused her attention – and then she gasped.

It was her name. Not her full name, just Adena, and the advertisement ended with *Marquis.*

Hands shaking so that the paper rustled noisily, Adena lowered it down onto the table and took a deep breath before she attempted to read it again.

On the hunt for the marooned Adena

Do you know a Miss Adena, recently missing for one night?

Do you know a Miss Adena with flaming red hair and sparkling green eyes?

Do you know a Miss Adena with astronomical knowledge, a fiery wit, and the ability to start fires?

If you do, a reward will be given to you for her full name and address.

She is owed an apology for stupidity and a very important question.

Contact the editor and ask for the Marquis.

Adena found that she was barely breathing, and

took a hasty gulp.

Well. She could never have predicted such a bold move, even from Luke. Her heart warmed at the very thought of his name, a name that she had vowed she would never speak again.

But how could she not? Her eyes scanned the advertisement once more: *She is owed an apology for stupidity and a very important question.*

Could that mean...? Her heart tried to prevent hope rising, but it was impossible. What a brave thing he had done, placing that there – opening himself up to ridicule perhaps, for there were only a few young marquis who would be searching to apologise to young ladies.

An apology for stupidity. To be sure, that was right: he had been stupid, to mislead her about the island. But then, so had she. Her own stupidity was of a different nature: she would not listen to him, she had not allowed him to explain.

Could he love her? Could there be any doubt after reading such an advertisement?

Ripping out the page of the newspaper and earning scandalised looks from the other patrons of the coffee house, Adena stuffed it into her reticule and made for the door.

She had a letter to write.

CHAPTER 10

*A*dena took a deep breath, and tried to prevent herself from rising and checking at the window again. He would come. Surely, he would come. The letter she had sent two days ago had specified this day, this time.

"Was it seven o'clock, you said?" Mrs Kerr was wearing a travelling cloak over a beautiful silk gown, along with an anxious expression.

Adena nodded. "Yes, Mrs Kerr, and please do not worry – you and Mr Kerr go and enjoy the ball. I am quite content to wait here for…for my friend. Is Rowena going with you?"

"She said that she would, but she is not dressed yet, head full of air at the moment," said Mrs Kerr fretfully, hovering by the door as though unsure whether she should allow herself to depart and leave her daughter's friend alone again. "You are staying here, in the house?"

Adena tried to smile and keep her irritation below the surface. It was perfectly natural for Rowena's mother to be anxious about leaving her alone – why, the last time that she had permitted her to be alone, she had gone missing an entire night.

"I assure you, Mrs Kerr, I have absolutely no intention of leaving the house until tomorrow for church," she said demurely, her hands folded respectfully on her lap. "I only wish to assure…my friend that I have returned to you safe and well. I am sure that they will not stay for long, and then I shall almost certainly retire for an early night."

Mrs Kerr's shoulders relaxed, and she smiled nervously. "Well, in that case I shall leave you – but remember that we are only two miles away, any of the footman can reach us if necessary, and – "

"My love, we shall be late." Her husband's voice interrupted her from the hallway.

"Go," said Adena gently. "I shall be here tomorrow morning for breakfast, you just see."

There was another moment's indecision on her hostess' face, but the steps of another person descending the stairs seemed to move her.

"Rowena, is that you?"

The door closed behind her as she moved into the hallway, but not before Adena caught the gentle admonishment of a parent to a slow and late child.

Adena smiled. Within a few minutes, they would all be out of the house – she could hardly have planned it better if she had tried! Soon, Luke would be here, and then…

But that was where her imagination petered out. Just exactly what was he going to say to her – and what would she say to him? She blushed at the ideas that ran through her mind. How brazen was she willing to be?

Time seemed to slip by very slowly as she waited for seven o'clock to arrive. Twice she rose to check that the small carriage clock on top of the bookcase in the drawing room was still running. At last, the slightly fast grandfather clock in the hallway began to chime the hour.

And nothing happened. Adena almost laughed aloud at the disappointment of it all: had she really thought that Luke would suddenly stride into the room as the last chime sounded? This was reality, not a fairy tale, she reminded herself. There may not be a happily ever after.

A knock at the door made her jump. "Yes?"

Bowing his entrance, a footman said gravely, "A gentleman to see you, my lady."

Adena swallowed. This was it. This was the moment that would decide her fate, and she felt as ill-prepared to face him as she had done two days ago, when she had sent off her letter.

"Send him in, please," was all that she could manage before she rose hastily to greet her guest.

Luke, Marquis of Dewsbury, looked even handsomer than she had remembered. Perhaps it was because he was dressed in the smartest clothes she had ever seen. Perhaps it was because she had not seen him for almost four days. Perhaps, and most likely, it was because he looked haughtily anxious, and it set off his looks perfectly.

Adena felt her heart begin to flutter, and she tried to swallow but found her throat was dry.

"My lady, my lord," the footman muttered as he closed the door behind him, and the snap caused them both to jump.

There can only be a few feet between us, Adena thought wildly. A few feet that he could cross in a few steps, if he wanted to. If he wanted to take me into his arms and kiss me, he need only step out.

He did not. Luke appeared to be as confused

and anxious as she was, and in no mood at all to get to the point.

"He called you 'my lady'," he said awkwardly, after bowing and receiving her curtsey. "Do you… do you have a title that I should know about?"

Adena laughed but stopped it quickly. "No, not at all. The Kerrs struggled to teach their footmen the social structure of the nobility and the correct introductions, so they have been taught to refer to all gentleman as 'my lord' and all ladies as 'my lady'."

She gestured that he should take a seat with one hand, but he ignored it.

"I…I need to say something first."

Adena's heart began to quicken, but she would not allow herself to be overcome, she simply would not. "I was surprised to see your advertisement in the paper – a rather ingenious idea."

Luke shrugged, but there was a hint of a smile on his lips. "I cannot claim it as my own, sadly, but I am certainly impressed by…by its efficacy."

Adena bit her lip. What was she supposed to say to that?

"The weather has been particular fine for this time of year," Luke garbled suddenly, eyes sparkling. "I should not have expected it to be so, considering – "

Adena sighed. This attempt at formal conversation was intolerable. She had to put an end to it.

"Luke," she said quietly, "I think we have come far enough in our…acquaintance, for want of a better word, to pass over the conversation about the weather, do you not?"

Whatever reaction she had expected her words to elicit, it was certainly not the one that occurred. Without another word, Luke dropped to his knees, and hung his head.

"Oh, Adena, how can I ever apologise enough?" He cried. "I look back at my actions and I wonder that I was ever able to even think of hiding the truth from you – my desire to know you should have been put aside for it was selfishness, and nothing else that made me keep you to myself for that night!"

Adena, startled beyond her wits and pleased to at least see some true feeling, tried to speak, but found her lungs simply did not have the power of speech.

"I do not think it will ever be possible for me to forgive myself," Luke said darkly from the floor, seemingly unable to raise his eyes to hers. "From the moment that you laughed at me over that fish – which I would also like to take this opportunity to apologise for, by the way – I knew that I wanted to marry you. That there was no one else that I could traverse through life with. But how could I speak, knowing the lie in which our entire acquaintance began?"

Now it was almost impossible for Adena to breathe, but she managed it, standing before him, watching the man she loved pour out his horror and sadness at his own actions.

That she would accept him, would marry him and become his wife, she had no doubt. The only question now was how long it would be before he gave her the chance to accept.

"I cannot grovel enough, and trust me, I am not a groveller," Luke was saying, finally able to raise his eyes to hers. She was startled to find that they were full of tears. "Can you imagine how it feels to know that you have discovered the greatest happiness that you will ever know, but that you have also forfeited it by a small decision made before you knew its value?"

Adena stared at him. He truly felt for her, that much was now evident: he cared for her, loved her even, though the words had not yet been said. Her heart swelled to see him, cried out in joy to hear his words.

"I...I love you, Adena." Luke swallowed and seemed to regain his courage to continue. "Those are words that I should have said to you before I made love to you, for I knew them to be true then, but I thought...well, 'tis shameful to admit as a gentleman, but I was afraid that my feelings would not be returned."

"Not be returned?" Adena managed hoarsely, but she was immediately interrupted.

"I knew it, I knew that you could not love me." Luke rose, a wretched look on his face that hurt Adena to her very core. "I will leave you now – I was so concerned that you may not have found your way back to your friends' protection, but I...I can leave you now, knowing that you are safe. By God, but it kills me to do it!"

He turned away from her, taking a stride towards the door but not before Adena had darted forward and placed herself before it, staring up at him resolutely.

"You would leave without hearing my answer?"

Luke stared at her, his eyes wild, his hair looking like it had not been tended to in days. "Answer?"

Adena could not help but smile now. They were

going to be so happy. "Yes, my answer. To your question."

"Question?" Luke did not appear to have any comprehension of what she was saying, but he stood still staring at her, eager for her words. "What question? Ah, whether you can forgive me or not? I hope you can, for if you cannot I will – "

Taking a step forward so that she was but inches from him, Adena whispered. "Hush your nonsense, Luke, Marquis of Dewsbury. For all your fancy title, you are sometimes very stupid."

His eyes widened and his mouth fell open, and it was so tempting that she did not even bother to try and fight it. Leaning forward, she kissed him full on the mouth.

She thought at first that Luke had frozen, but then large and warm hands were clinging to her waist, and she was almost lifted upwards in the power of his embrace as he returned her kiss devotedly.

How long they stood there, she could not tell. All Adena knew was that when they broke apart, she had just enough breath to say, "This time, I know my own way back to shore. Luke, I love you."

He did not need to reply in words: his actions were enough. Stepping forward with such passion that Adena was forced to step backwards, Luke pinned her against the door and took full possession of her mouth as his hands returned to her hips, that favourite place.

They could have spent all night there, murmuring love and affection betwixt the sweetest of kisses, but as Luke clutched at her even more tightly, Adena felt a familiar hardness between his legs.

Luke dropped his face down with an almost embarrassed smile. "Look at what you do to me, you brazen woman."

"I would say you are the one who is brazen," Adena corrected him, returning his smile. "This time, it is I who will lead you. Come, follow me."

She forced him to take a step backwards so she could open the door, and they stepped into the empty hallway.

"Where are we going?" Luke asked, with a hint of confusion and nervousness in his voice

Adena smiled. "Why, to my bedchamber of course. Have you not been longing to make love to me on an actual bed?"

It was fortunate that there was no painting hanging on the wall just outside the drawing room door, for they would surely have knocked it from the wall as Luke thrust her against the wall and kissed her neck with such fervour that Adena gasped aloud.

"Adena, you temptress, we cannot," Luke groaned heavily against her neck as she entwined her hands around his neck.

"Why not?" She returned in a whisper, allowing a mischievous smile to dance across her face. "Rowena and her parents are away this evening, at a ball a few miles away. All but one maid and a footman are gone, and they are surely busy. We are completely alone."

Luke hesitated for a moment and stared into her eyes, as though attempting to read her thoughts. Finally he said, "You truly want this?"

Adena smiled. "Am I to be your wife?"

"How can you ask that?"

"And I would ask the same question," she returned swiftly, and taking one of his hands in hers, brought it to her breast.

Luke groaned once more, and muttered, "Lead the way then, Adena, or I shall take you right here on this floor, and then God help us!"

Laughing, Adena ran up the stairs with her love in hot pursuit. They almost made it to her bedroom without succumbing to their desire to taste each other once again, and Luke almost had his shirt removed by the time that they finally shut the door behind them and enclosed themselves in a true sanctuary.

It did not stay on for long. Adena ran her fingers over his collarbone, down the wiry hair across his chest, and moaned quietly.

"I did not have the chance to take a proper look at you before," she whispered. "My, but I had missed out!"

"And so have I," said Luke in a growl. "I want to spend our entire honeymoon completely naked, just enjoying the sight of you."

Adena laughed. "Enough talk, we have the rest of our lives to talk."

She pulled him towards the bed and fell on top of him, her hair falling over him like a fire.

"We have the rest of our lives to do this, too," he pointed out, but she claimed his mouth with her own.

"Perhaps," she said eventually. "But right now, I want you more than I want your conversation."

She could feel the damp heat between her legs again, and this time, she knew what delights were in store for her. Arching her back upwards, she gave a little moan as Luke nuzzled his way down her neck and towards those tempting breasts, barely hidden now as they hung heavy towards him.

"I love you," he murmured as he rolled her onto her back. "I love you so much."

Adena took in his swollen lips, swollen from the fierceness of his passion, the darkness of the stubble on his cheeks, thicker now since when she had first beheld it, and felt the hardness of his desire pushing up through his britches, through her gown.

"I have to – I have to have you now!" She gasped.

Luke smiled, and gently pulled at the ribbon to allow her gown to fall open, revealing her heaving breasts. "There is plenty of time for that – I want to make this last for you."

But Adena was having none of that. Rolling over once more, she straddled him and stared at him fiercely, fiery red hair flowing down her neck and grazing her nipples as her gown fell open.

"No," she said firmly, panting slightly. "I want you now. Right now, Luke!"

WHO WAS he to say no? He could have taken her up against the wall downstairs in that drawing room if he had allowed himself to be overcome by his desire for her, and he was in no position to protest.

"Sit up on your knees," Luke instructed her, and moaned aloud as the movement made her breasts jiggle up and down. He tugged at his britches and pulled them off, lying beneath her completely naked. "Now come here."

Adena lowered herself down, slowly at first as though frightened of hurting him, but she soon settled happily on him as she glorified in the feeling of his hardness against her softness.

"I do not know – I do not know what to do," she mumbled, eyes wide with confusion but completely trusting.

Luke grinned. "Instinct will take over, after a point. Here."

He sat up and brought one of those stunning nipples into his mouth, and she cried out with the sensation of it, causing him to jerk and stiffen even more. She was kissing his head and clutching at his back, almost scratching him with the uncontrolled pleasure that she was experiencing, and Luke grasped at the other breast to intensify it for her.

She was growing wetter, wetter than before – the anticipation was growing in her, now that Adena knew what delights he had in store for her.

He was almost slick with it, and in a swift movement his hands grasped at her bottom under the billowing skirts, and raised her onto him.

"Oh!" Adena's eyes widened as she felt him enter her, but there was no pain there; he had made sure of that with the near climax he had given her through her breasts. "Oh, Luke!"

Tilting his face up, she leaned down and kissed him passionately, and for a moment he allowed her to stay there, straddling him and encompassing him in her tightness. But eventually he could not stop himself, and he allowed his hands to move to her waist underneath her gown, groaning into her mouth at the feeling of her sweet flesh.

Now that his hands were not restraining her, Adena's hips naturally began to move, the kiss working up in her the instincts that Luke knew would take over.

It was impossible to remain upright, he simply couldn't do it. Luke fell backwards on the bed but Adena was now in her stride, rising and falling, rising and falling and he could not take his eyes off her beautiful face and bouncing breasts.

"God, Adena, I love you!" Luke groaned. "Yes, faster, faster!"

She did not seem able to hear him, her eyes

were closed with the ecstasy of the feeling of him, but this time she was in complete control, and she slowed down slightly with a growing smile.

"No, Adena – oh God, you wanted it now, take me!"

Luke had never considered himself as someone to beg. He never had before – and he never would with anyone else. But this was Adena, sweetest gift of his life, and ardently possessive woman.

She was the one in control now.

"I can feel it building," Adena cried, and her eyes snapped open. "Oh, Luke, I can feel it!"

"Let it happen," he shouted, "Adena, yes, yes!"

They came together, and it was almost like a cascade of climax that swept them both aside, leaving them nothing but pure and delightful sensations that overwhelmed them both.

After a period of time that Luke could not even have guessed at, Adena collapsed onto his chest, her breasts heavy and her breath short.

"That," she whimpered, "was incredible."

Luke tried to catch his breath, and laughed. "And it will not be our last."

There had been little conversation after that. Neither of them had the brainpower for it, but at mutual agreement, they both stripped off what little clothes they still had on, and nestled under the blankets, completely naked, as happily as if the vicar had already declared them man and wife.

For, as Luke said, could they be more to each other than husband and wife?

Luke fell asleep quickly, but he was in for a rude awakening. Not five hours after their eyes had succumbed to sleep, a raucous banging was heard from the hallway.

"Adena? Adena, wake up!"

Luke awoke with a jolt, and stared wide-eyed and panicked at Adena.

"The Kerrs!" She whispered horrified. "They are back – and they want me?"

"What should I do?" Luke whispered anxiously. "I am completely naked here, Adena, I have no time to dress and hide!"

"Then just hide," said Adena firmly. "My dressing room, go!"

Grasping at his clothes and moving as quickly and quietly as he could through the door at which Adena pointed, Luke closed it with a snap, seconds before a loud bang declared that Adena's bedroom door had been thrown open.

"Is she here?" Luke heard a woman's voice cry out in panic, and then Adena's reply.

"Who?"

"Rowena, of course!" The woman must be Mrs Kerr, Luke guessed. Why was she looking for her daughter in Adena's bedchamber?

It appeared that Adena had a similar question. "Why would Rowena be here, I thought she was with you?"

There were more bangs in the house, and Luke tried desperately to dress himself without making a sound.

"She has gone!" The woman's voice sounded hysterical. "She has gone, Adena, and look – she has left a note!"

Luke paused, half in, half out of his britches. Gone?

"My dearest parents, do not be alarmed," he heard Adena's voice as she read. "I am quite well and safe, and have gone...have gone to Gretna Green to be married – "

The woman who must surely be Mrs Kerr cried out in a dry sob.

" – married at once, so there is no hope in attempting to follow me," Adena's voice continued. "My God, Mrs Kerr, you must after her at once!"

"That is where her father has gone – he is to

London in the carriage, but I thought she may be with you!"

Luke pulled his britches up and buttoned them. Well, well: an elopement in the house.

"Go and ride to the coach house," he heard Adena say. "Or better yet, go there yourself! Find out which coach they got, whither it was bound!"

"Yes," murmured the voice distracted for a moment. "That is a sound idea, Miss Garland – you do not mind if we take the servants with us? You will be quite alone for the rest of the night, but we could ask door to door, see if – "

"That is an excellent idea," came Adena's firm tone, and Luke grinned. He did not need to see her to know that look. "I will stay here, in case she comes back."

"Bless you child, bless you!"

There was another slam of a door, a moment of silence, and then: "Luke?"

Luke quietly opened the door back into the bedroom, and crept into bed with his fiancée. "An elopement and an engagement, all in the same night!"

Adena welcomed him with open arms, and snuggled into him. "Indeed. We shall have to be up at the crack of dawn to start looking for her."

Luke sighed. "Life is never going to be dull with you, is it?"

He caught the answering smile on Adena's lips, and it warmed his heart like nothing else.

"No," she admitted, grinning. "But as long as we are never marooned again, I think we will do quite well."

"And even then," he murmured in her ear, drawing her close.

Adena sighed. "Even then."

*Worried about Rowena? Fear not — you can read her
Ravishing Regencies story in* Voyage with a Viscount *—
read on for the first chapter…
Please do leave a review if you have enjoyed this book — I love
reading your thoughts, comments, and even critiques!
You can also receive my news, special offers, and updates by
signing up to my mailing list at*
www.subscribepage.com/emilymurdoch

VOYAGE WITH A VISCOUNT

CHAPTER ONE

Rowena Kerr did not think anything could disgust her more than Oscar Bentley, and then she saw the rain.

"Why in God's name did you not mention this earlier?" She asked him quietly, barely audible over the din of the crashing rain that was splashing over their feet as they stood in the doorway of the inn.

Mr Bentley shrugged, a pink tinge of embarrassment covering his face, almost unable to meet her eye.

Rowena rolled her eyes. What a complete idiot – and they had come all this way for…well, there was nothing for it now.

Striding forwards without giving Mr Bentley

another glance, Rowena stepped into the pouring rain.

Within seconds her hair was wet through, her clothes damp, but it was better than standing beside him any longer. She could not bare to look at him, to be near him, and she hated herself for believing – as she had mere hours before – that she could. By God, had she known…

"Miss Kerr!"

The idiot had followed her out into the thrashing rain, blinking away the drops that fell into his eyes.

"Miss Kerr, I – " But he stopped off short, likely horrified by the fierce glare that she bestowed upon him. Her father had always said that she could stare down a bull, and it looked like he was right. Mr Bentley at least was instantly cowed, and took a slippery step backwards in the mud.

Rowena looked around her. She had barely taken in their location when they had arrived, had just been glad to get out of that coach which had bounced and thrown them about for miles on end. So here they were, at the Wingston Inn. Miles from anywhere, with nothing but hills and a few trees in any direction. A grubby track went past it, but no coaches were visible.

"You…you cannot stand out here, Miss Kerr."

She ignored him. Cold, she may be, anxious and upset, definitely, but this feeling of foolishness was nothing to do with the weather. How could she have done it? What had she been thinking?

"Pasty, dear?"

Rowena jumped at the close sound of another, and saw an elderly woman with a basket on her arm covered by a patchwork cloth, and shook her head hastily.

No, the last thing that she wants is a conversation. "Thank you, but I am just waiting for a coach. I have no need for sustenance."

Without waiting for a reply, and in a manner that Rowena knew was rudeness itself but she simply could not help it, she had to move away.

Mr Bentley had not returned inside the Wingston Inn, though. He was still standing there, undoubtedly as wet through as she was, staring at her with a strange mixture of longing and confusion.

Rowena coloured slightly, and tried to ignore him, but his constant stare and cold, dejected manner was difficult not to see.

Just when her feet were starting to grow damp through her leather boots, Rowena's heart leapt: a coach. Surely that was a coach that she could hear? Within minutes, her hopes were confirmed as a large stagecoach came rattling around a corner and pulled up outside the Wingston Inn.

Three people dismounted, stretching their arms, twisting their backs, obviously delighted to be free of the coach – but they were barely able to take two steps away from it before Rowena rushed forward.

"Good day – good day, where is this coach going to? Where is its next destination?"

Most of the previous occupants pushed past her, desperate to get out of the thrashing rain and into the dry, warm, and hopefully food-filled air of the Wingston Inn, but Rowena clutched at the driver's arm.

"You must tell me. Where will this coach take me?"

She dropped the man's arm quickly when he saw the leering smile that he gave her, his eyes moving up and down her body. Rowena smiled nervously, and wished that she had thought to put a coat on. Her gown, a deep rich purple in the dry, was now almost black, and clung to her body in a most disgraceful way.

"This coach, girlie?" The coachman sniggered. "Anywhere you want it to go, my sweet."

Rowena coloured, and held herself a little more upright as she repeated, "Where will this coach take me?"

She did not attempt to use an aristocratic eye very often, but her striking features and undeniable beauty was not something to be ignored.

The coachman dropped his eyes. "Aylesbury, my lady."

Rowena tried not to let the disappointment wash over her, so she nodded, and then strode over to the forlorn and stupid Mr Bentley.

"I must admit myself disappointed for the second time today," she said curtly. "This coach is departing for the opposite way from which I would like to go – but you, Mr Bentley, should embark immediately. Is that not towards your home?"

"I – I must say," Mr Bentley spluttered, hands clasped together and eyes beseeching, "No apology can be sufficient, Miss Kerr, I understand that, but if you could understand just how sorry I am, perhaps you would find it in your heart to forgive – "

"Get on the coach," said Rowena, rolling her eyes as she stared across the sodden ground to the only coach that seemed likely to arrive today. "And tell no one – no one, mark me Bentley – of what has happened here. If I find that you have…"

She did not need to finish her sentence: he knew exactly what power she held over him. He would say nothing.

Rowena felt the rain finally reach her skin as she stood and watched Mr Bentley silent clamber into the coach. An awkward parting, that was true, but a necessary one. If she were honest with herself, she was relieved to see him go.

The coach did not linger for long. Within five minutes, it was trundling away from the Wingston Inn in the same direction from which it came, and Rowena felt a weight lift from her shoulders.

She was still wet, and was now growing cold, but at least he was gone.

"My lady, will you not come inside?"

Rowena turned to see the proprietor of the Wingston Inn standing in the doorway, staring at her standing there in the rain.

She shook her head. "I am waiting for the coach to Marshurst – or anywhere near it."

The man sighed, and beckoned her in once more. "That coach will not be here for two days, my lady – come, into the warm."

Rowena's shoulders slumped, and she groaned aloud as her eyes tracked an elaborately decorated coach pull up to the Wingston Inn. Another two days?

James, Viscount Paendly, was jerked awake as the coach he was sleeping in made an abrupt stop, and he groaned.

To think he was still in this godforsaken coach – how long had it been now, five days? Six? Had no man suffered as deeply as himself? There was surely no one who could commiserate fully with the boredom he was encountering. Such a long journey, with nothing to do, nothing to see, and nothing to look forward to when he arrives.

Sleep was the only refuge for the truly bored, he reflected with a sardonic smile as he pulled his greatcoat around his shoulders. But then, when you lived a boring life as he did, there was little change of scenery when you spent the best part of a week trapped in a rattling box on wheels.

Yes indeed, life was boring – but it was the title that did that. Duties, responsibilities, actions: but no joy. No mirth, no opportunity for frivolity, or revelling. No, the Viscount Paendly had to be serious, had to be dependable. You could not have the Viscount Paendly doing anything interesting.

It was why he had jumped to help her, of course, but now Giselle was off, and back to France, there was nothing to do but return to his boring existence.

James glanced out of the window, and saw nothing but a grey dull inn, stained brown with rain and mud.

Was there ever a man more desperate for excitement than himself? James shook his head bitterly. One only had to think of his friend Pierre, and the ridiculous excitement that he had enjoyed recently – an escape from France, a woman in his life to shock him and force him out of banality!

By God, if he could procure a similar adventure for himself.

James blinked, and brought the sad damp inn back into focus. There was someone there, standing outside the inn with no thought for the driving rain that had been the companion of all travellers for nigh on twenty minutes.

It was a woman.

James leaned unconsciously towards the

opening in his carriage, and saw the dejected expression on her features. She was dishevelled and wet, to be sure, but he had rarely seen a person hold themselves with such elegance.

The more he looked, the more he saw. Her clothes were rich, and she evidently came from some wealth. He could not see her features closely, as she kept turning to argue with a man who was standing just inside the dry, by the door of the inn.

He could not hear their words, but the root of their conversation was clear enough: she wanted to be left alone, and yet the man continued to force his conversation on her.

A strange feeling of impulse began to creep over him.

James shook his head with a smile. No, he needed to fight that unusual feeling: he was not the man to randomly act. Everything for him was calculated, planned in advance, prepared carefully. Was that not what being the Viscount Paendly was all about?

But the desire was growing in him, out of character as it may be, but the need to do something different, something totally unlike what he had ever done before was overwhelming.

Before he really knew what he was doing, James

had pushed open the door of the carriage, dropped onto the mud with his nice clean boots, and strode over to her.

The closer that he got the easier it was to see her expression – now startled at his approach. James' jaw dropped: never before had he seen such bedraggled beauty. It was enough to amaze him, and he had seen much of the world.

"What exactly seems to be the problem?" He found himself saying, glancing between this stunning young woman, and a gentleman of definitely lower rank who had bowed deeply as he approached.

In a low murmur, the man said with a grovelling smile, "My lord, I was merely offering the lady some refreshment and shelter, but she is adamant that she will wait outside for a coach – a coach, moreover, that goes in the Marshurst direction, and I have informed her will not be here for another two days."

James found that as the man spoke, his gaze meandered over to the woman. Captured by her beauty, he was astounded to find that she was staring back at him defiantly, with no coquettish blush on her cheeks, no gentle turn of the head to display her neck in the most elegant fashion. No, she was doing nothing but glaring at him.

"And as you can see, my lord," the man was continuing to bleat, "the weather being what it is, I wanted to ensure that the lady – "

"I am going in that direction." For a moment, James was unsure exactly who had spoken, but the way that both the woman and the innkeeper were staring at him, the words must have come from his own lips. "I can take you half the way."

What was he doing? Had he gone mad, to be accepting stowaways onto his coach?

But James did not feel mad. He felt more alive than he had done in weeks, and he watched the young woman, soaking wet as she was, hesitate to reply to his offer.

He saw the clenching of her jaw, the way her eyes flickered over him, attempting perhaps to guess at his class and therefore his honour, and found himself silently hoping that she would accept his offer.

"I – I thank you," she eventually said stiffly, and James marvelled at the softness of her tone. "I would be most grateful for any distance that you can take me."

"My lady!" The innkeeper looked affronted, and he glared at James as the cause for the loss of a potential customer. "You know this gentleman?"

James glanced at the woman, who shook her head without taking her eyes from him.

"And you will step into his carriage, without even knowing his name?" The man sounded aghast, but his words lit a fire in James' stomach and caused him to grin.

"All part of the adventure," he found himself saying with a shrug. Moving quickly forward, he grasped the one piece of luggage that sat in the mud beside the young lady, and offered his arm to her.

There was another moment's hesitation, and James felt his heart thundering in his chest. This was unlike anything he had ever done, or will do again in all likelihood. Why not play the part of rescuer to perfection?

But the woman he was rescuing did not seem to have any idea of letting him have his own way entirely. With a contemptuous look at the innkeeper, and a raised eyebrow at James' arm, she strode ahead of him and was in the carriage in a trice.

A flicker of excitement rose in James' chest.

This woman was unlike anyone he had ever met — and there was plenty of adventure left in the road.

Without saying another word to the innkeeper, James, Viscount Paendly, followed his new travelling companion into the carriage.

HISTORICAL NOTE

I always strive for accuracy with my historical books, as a historian myself, and I have done my best to make my research pertinent and accurate. Any mistakes that have slipped in must be forgiven, as I am but a lover of this era, not an expert.

ABOUT THE AUTHOR

Emily Murdoch is a historian and writer. Throughout her career so far she has examined a codex and transcribed medieval sermons at the Bodleian Library in Oxford, designed part of an exhibition for the Yorkshire Museum, worked as a researcher for a BBC documentary presented by Ian Hislop, and worked at Polesden Lacey with the National Trust. She has a degree in History and English, and a Masters in Medieval Studies, both from the University of York. Emily has a medieval series, a Regency series, and a Western series published, and is currently working on several new projects.

You can follow her on twitter and instagram @emilyekmurdoch, find her on facebook at www.-facebook.com/theemilyekmurdoch, and read her blog at www.emilyekmurdoch.com

Made in the USA
Middletown, DE
10 July 2019